SCARS

An Amazing End-Times Prophecy Novel

By Patience Prence

Spring Harvest
UNITED STATES OF AMERICA

SCARS

By Patience Prence

www.thespringharvest.com

Published by
Spring Harvest U.S.A.

ISBN 978-0-9826336-0-1

For Yeshua

And it shall come to pass in the last days, saith God, I will pour out of my Spirit upon all flesh: and your sons and your daughters shall prophesy, and your young men shall see visions, and your old men shall dream dreams.

Acts 2:17

TABLE OF CONTENTS

1

THE DREAM

The primeval recesses of her soul clinch with terror.

Instinct screams at her, pushes her to get away, to survive before it is too late.

Becky's innocent gaze darts across the landscape. All she sees are the dark outline of mounds of dirt and massive oak trees in the distance.

Her small white hands clutch at her pink-flowered nightgown.

RUN! her mind screams over and over again.

She slowly inhales a trembling breath and wills her legs to move forward. She darts out of the line of prisoners that has just descended from the train. She sprints past the rusty boxcars and the three soldiers clad in black, grasping machine guns.

A whistle screeches, and large circles of bright lights dance with the shadows around the expansive train yard.

Cold air stings her lungs as they pump her panicked breath past her chapped lips. Her racing blood echoes in her ears. Beyond a final set of iron tracks, a dark field stretches out before her.

Her muscles burn as she pushes her legs to move faster and harder toward the safety of the trees on the other side of the field. Cold wind whips at her flushed face.

RUN! her mind screams as she obeys its command.

Sagebrush cuts into her legs. Jagged rocks puncture her bare feet. Her heart wants to explode in her chest.

A mustard-colored bulldozer with its broad hydraulic blade sits like a sleeping dinosaur in the darkness ahead.

She runs to the far side of the metal heap and braces her palms against the worn rusty tracks. The bloody soles of her feet throb with pain. Her legs tremble uncontrollably. She tries to quiet her stinging breath.

The glint of a flashlight beam ricochets against the cold, yellow steel of the bulldozer. Her eyes widen at the sound of heavy footsteps.

She buries her pain and hurries into the shadows.

Her ankle twists under her weight, and she falls on her hands and knees. A hill of fresh dirt looms before her. Impetuously she crawls to the mound.

A putrid stench rises from a large dark pit next to the mound. "UGH!" Her nose wrinkles in disgust.

Sharp gravel tears at her flimsy nightgown as she rolls down the side into the pit. Her body becomes light as it falls into the darkness below. Her back slams hard against the moist ground, knocking the wind out of her. Dazed, she stares up at the cold night sky blanketed with stars.

Loud sirens puncture the chill of the night air. Clutching her knees tight to her chest, she folds herself into the blackest corner of the pit trying to make herself invisible.

Long minutes pass as she strains to make sense of the noises above her. Deep, male voices call out to each other across the crisp sky; boots fall heavily against gravel; gun metal rattles sharply.

Without warning a diesel engine roars to life, smothering all the other sounds.

She feels a grip of fear in the core of her stomach.

All around her the ground begins to vibrate. The heavy machine groans and lumbers toward the pit. Small rocks and soil cascade from the stars above.

"*OH, NO!*" Becky screams under her breath as the wailing of the bulldozer grows louder and louder.

I've got to get out of here—or I'll be buried alive! Her fingernails claw at the steep earthen walls of the pit as she tries to exit her hiding place. The metal beast roars and shakes the ground. The walls of the pit crumble in. Becky falls backward as an ocean of dirt and rocks crashes on top of her. The weight of the rubble presses hard against her small chest.

Dirt fills her mouth and her eyes.

HELP ME! PLEASE HELP ME! she wants to scream at the top of her lungs, but only mud sputters from her mouth. Her arms flail against the raining debris.

I can't see. . .I can't breathe. . . .

Her fingers brush the familiar shape of a human hand. Her heart speeds as she grabs hold like a drowning girl grasping for a life preserver. Through the suffocating grime and darkness she searches for the face belonging to the hand that would rescue her and pull her from the choking bowels of the earth.

The bulldozer growls again. The walls of the pit melt inward. The earth holds Becky's weak body in a paralyzing grip. She helplessly stops fighting against it and holds onto the hand with all her remaining strength. As the walls of the pit collapse, they release the body of a young man from his grave. He rolls with the heaving ground and settles next to Becky like a limp rag doll. His black, hollow eyes stare back at her.

Becky's eyelids fling open as she springs awake with a jolt.

The weight of the earth still presses down on her chest. She hears the pounding of her heart in her ears. She sits up and wipes the perspiration off her forehead with her clammy hands. Her blanket is damp with sweat. She realizes she has just had another horrible nightmare about that awful prison death camp.

Scarlet moonlight casts an eerie glow through the barred window.

"I wonder what time it is," she whispers under her breath.

No one answers.

A dry breeze moves the tree outside her window. Its shadow revolves along the bare walls.

Becky lays her head back down on her flat, soiled pillow. She visualizes the trains rolling by. She can see the faces, gaunt with hunger and fear, looking out at her from the boxcars. Even in the waking world those despondent eyes still plead with her.

The images move across her mind over and over like a movie she cannot turn off. She doesn't want to turn it off. Someone has to remember what the World Union has done to them.

The trains roll by again, slowly, one after another; their heavy loads creak against the steel tracks: click, clack, click, clack. Ashen, scared faces peer down at her as they pass by, one after another.

She hears Peter Roma's frantic voice boom from the loudspeakers and reverberate off the marble walls of Saint Peter's Square in Rome. "These resisters and intolerant fundamentalists are the cause of all the death and destruction of the earth, and because of their disobedience to the Christ they all must be eliminated. . . ."

In the back of her mind she agonizes over one inescapable question: *When will they take me to my death?¹*

She fills the long, hot days with memories. Memories are all that are left to her.

The cell walls illuminate shades of gold and red as the morning sun peeks from the east.

Becky leans back on her pillow and closes her eyes. "Thank You, Lord Jesus," she whispers quietly. "Thank You for another day. I'm so happy to know You--the real Jesus! Amen."

Soon the guard will bring me my breakfast. Becky's empty stomach growls at the thought of food.

She flings back the cover and sits up. The cot squeaks loudly as she rolls off the lumpy mattress and plants both feet on the hard bare floor.

Her thin hands flatten the wrinkled, baggy shirt that hangs on her like a dress.

When she arrived here she traded in her pink-flowered nightgown for the bright orange shirt and pants of a prisoner. The pants are too big, intended for a male, so she wears only the shirt.

The dirty floor thumps as she crosses the room to the small tiled bathroom.

The girl staring back at her from the large mirror over the sink looks so much older than sixteen. Dark circles lie under her baby-blue eyes. They're her mother's eyes. Looking into the reflection, she easily conjures the image of her mother. She can clearly see Momma walking through the front door of their home, returning from work, her purple scrubs clinging to her fake breasts and her long

---

¹ "Blessed are they which are persecuted for righteousness' sake: for theirs is the kingdom of heaven" (Matthew 5:10).

blond hair falling neatly in a French braid down the middle of her back. The thought of Momma pierces Becky's heart.

Men always liked Momma. She carried herself with confidence on a tall Nordic frame. Her dazzling blue eyes could smolder or tease at her will. Despite the wedding ring on her finger, men often hit up on her. The doctors at Orange Valley Community Hospital where she worked as a licensed volunteer nurse were no exception.

"You are such a pretty girl," Momma would whisper in the quiet evenings as they sat on the edge of Becky's bed. Momma would run a round nylon brush down the length of her shiny blond hair.

"Oh, Momma." Becky would shake her head. "I'm not pretty! My nose is too big, and besides. . .you're just saying that because I'm your daughter!"

"Okay, Rebekah. . .then how did you become a cheerleader?" Momma asked. "Cheerleaders aren't ugly!"

Becky leans over, cups her hands and fills them with the warm, rusty liquid that streams from the faucet. She then splashes her face and rubs her teeth with her fingers to clean them.

She remembers standing before the panel of judges while nervously performing the routine she had practiced for weeks.

Her nose had almost kept her from trying out for the cheerleading squad. But, for as long as she could remember, when she imagined her future, she saw herself on the sidelines at the Lotus Bowl: kicking, smiling and dancing alongside the other beautiful cheerleaders, wearing the same sexy uniforms, knowing the whole union watched and admired her beauty and style. And that one guy in particular, Blake Collins, would not only admire her, but he would love her.

If her dreams of the future had any chance of coming true, she would have to take the first step of joining the cheerleading squad at Valley High School.

T.J. helped her practice. Every day after school she coached Becky through her routines. "Kick high! Come on, Becky—you own it, girlfriend! You are going to kick butt!"

Even with her mother's assurances that she was pretty and her best friend's encouragement, Becky still thought she was clumsy and awkward as she performed her routine in front of five of her teachers who made up the panel of judges at the tryouts.

When she found her name on the list posted on the gym door, she was elated. That was one of her happiest memories. T.J. squealed and jumped up and down and gave Becky a big bear hug. When Becky told Momma she had made the squad, Momma kissed her cheek and said, "I knew you could do it! I am so proud of you, Rebekah!"

Becky reaches up and touches her nose.

"You got your nose from your grandma Silver. You should be very proud. She was a good strong woman, and she gave you a good strong nose." The memory of her father's voice was so intense she could almost feel him standing next to her. A smile creeps across her face.

"What girl wants to look like her grandma?" she had said with a pout.

"Now, Princess." His lips curled up to form a smile. "Beauty's only skin deep; love is to the bone. Beauty gradually fades away, but ugly holds its own!"

Becky can feel the aching void in her chest as she remembers her dad's silly sayings. *Oh! How I miss Daddy. . . .*

When Daddy stood next to Momma they made the oddest couple. Momma was so tall and slender with a gorgeous figure and a very classy lady.

Daddy, he was short and stout. His big heart shone through his laughing brown eyes. His skin was dark from long, hard hours laboring in the sun as a building contractor. His T-shirt always needed pressing, and his tummy usually hung over his worn blue jeans concealing the top button that was always undone!

7

Becky's mind momentarily returns to her cell. As she stands in front of the mirror, she notices the contented smile on her reflection. She runs her fingers through her tangled hair. Despite her efforts at grooming, her long blond hair is still mussed and tangled.

She can hear her mom's soft voice. "Rebekah, you are so lucky to have such beautiful, long, blond hair. Other women pay a fortune to have their hair colored like yours!"

If Momma could only see it now, all matted and full of knots! I swear if I had scissors I would cut it all off!

Her smile fades as she yanks at the knots. She runs her fingers through her hair one last time. She grabs the drawstring from the orange pants she had left on the counter the night before and ties her hair back into a ponytail.

Somewhat satisfied with her look, she creeps back to her cot and eagerly waits for breakfast. Her meals are the only thing she looks forward to.

Soon the large metal door clangs, signaling the arrival of breakfast and the beginning of another daily cycle.

Outside her cell stands a guard at least six-foot tall. A white band with "W.U." in blue letters is wrapped around his bulging bicep on the arm of his khaki uniform.

Becky moves out of her cot and hurries toward the door. She notices a neatly wrapped white gauze bandage covers his right hand as he pushes the tray of food under the barred door.

"Thank you," she says, wondering if he understands English. She pitches her ponytail over her shoulder and reaches for the tray sitting on the floor.

The guard's light-blue beret bobs up and down as he acknowledges her with a silent nod and disappears down the dark, narrow hallway.

She crams a dry piece of burnt toast into her mouth and hurries back to her bed with the plastic yellow tray.

"Dear Jesus," she prays, eager for another bite of toast, "thanks again for another meal. Please bless this food, in Jesus' name, amen."

She consciously chews the black bread over and over again until it disappears in her mouth. She savors each and every bite of the bland, stale meal. She crunches down on the dry cereal and washes every last morsel down with a cup of watery orange juice.

She tries not to focus on the fact that her stomach is far from full as she shoves the empty, plastic tray back under the door. The guard will be back later to pick it up.

Following her routine, she returns to her cot and rests her head against her pillow. The sunlight bounces off the ground outside the window and plays on the water-stained, cottage-cheese ceiling of the small room.

The silence is unavoidable. Her mind works overtime to try to fill the emptiness.

She whispers prayers of hope that Jesus will return soon and destroy that imposter Peter Roma.

She recites Bible verses over and over in her mind as the sunlight moves steadily across the ceiling, marking minutes then hours. She finds comfort in the Scriptures and yet so many questions. How could millions of others not see the truth she had found in the Bible?[2] Why couldn't they see that Peter Roma was *not* Jesus of Nazareth and that the Bible warned of the coming false prophet?[3]

She was not so different from those who believed Peter Roma. She wasn't raised to be religious, and she hadn't known much about the rapture or Jesus of Nazareth.

Her parents were polar opposites even in their religious backgrounds. Her father, Joseph, was raised in a Jewish home, and her mother, Kirsten, was raised Catholic. But in their adulthood neither rigorously practiced their faith. A couple of times a year her father would take

---

[2]   "God will send them strong delusion, that they should believe the lie" (2 Thessalonians 2:11).

[3]   "Then I saw another beast coming up out of the earth, and he had two horns like a lamb and spoke like a dragon" (Revelation 13:11).

the family to synagogue services, and every year they celebrated the Passover. Whenever she heard a tragic story or passed a graveyard, her mother would make the sign of the cross. Her habit was so automatic that to Becky it resembled the practice of knocking on wood to ward off bad luck.

"We all worship the same God," her mother would explain whenever Becky questioned the difference in her parents' religions. "Some of us call him God[4]; others call him Allah or Buddha. Knowing his name isn't as important as knowing he wants you to be a good little girl," she would say with a wry wink.

The shadows slowly move across the walls. Her isolation is punctuated by the absence of sound. The only noises to penetrate her being are the incessant wind moving outside her window and the low whispers of her desperate prayers. She squeezes her eyes shut as the dusty light streams through the bars of her window. Her memories take her back to a place that changed her life forever. . . .

■■

It was a sunny, warm afternoon. Becky descended from the school bus and started walking the half block to her home. The wide, tree-lined streets of her Southern California suburb were unusually empty and quiet. The familiar sounds of the neighbor boys' skateboards rolling on the rough asphalt and clacking against every curb and low concrete wall were noticeably absent. So, too, were the occasional minivan and hybrid cars that reluctantly slowed and swerved to avoid hitting the skateboarders. A leaf blower and lawn mower stood abandoned in her neighbor's meticulously manicured front yard. She noticed the three Mexican gardeners gathered in the driveway around their old pickup truck. She waved to them, but they did not

---

[4] "Jesus saith unto him, I am the way, the truth, and the life: no man cometh unto the Father, but by me," (John 14:6).

notice her. They were intently focused on the frantic voice speaking through the Spanish language radio station.

Must be a big soccer game on today, she thought.

The scene that greeted her when she walked through the front door was equally disconcerting. Her mother, father and little brother, David, sat huddled on the tan leather couch transfixed.

"Hundreds of thousands, possibly millions, of people are dead. Many others are missing. It will be weeks before we know the full extent of the death and destruction that have just happened."

A look of distress in Momma's eyes startled Becky. "What's wrong?" she asked apprehensively.

"A big tsunami on the East Coast," her father said calmly without taking his eyes away from the television screen. "It hit a few hours ago. Looks like New York City and Miami were both hit pretty bad. They say the waves were over five hundred feet high."

Anchorwoman Suze Graham's familiar pretty green eyes were glazed with panic as she stared into the camera and robotically delivered the grim details.

"We have just now been able to establish contact with our reporter, Jose Ruiz, who is on the ground in Miami." She held her hand to her ear. "JOSE, CAN YOU HEAR ME?"

"YES, SUZE, I CAN HEAR YOU!" An image of Jose holding a black cordless microphone close to his mouth appeared on the television screen. "As you can see, I am standing in about three feet of water in downtown Miami. The scene is indescribable." His shaky voice crackled over the airwaves. "Bodies are floating everywhere, and the stench is unbearable. Sewage is obviously in this water. It is very dangerous to move around here. Debris is all over the place—broken glass, power lines. Oh, my. . . ." His words trailed off. "I don't believe it—there's a dead horse over there!" Jose shook his head as he pointed toward a large black mass in the brown polluted water. The camera flashed images of a black horse, his body bloated and his limbs paralyzed in a straight position.

"Everywhere you look is unbelievable destruction. Above me"—Jose pointed upward—"on the second story of this building is the tailgate of a pickup truck sticking out of the windows of JJ's Ice Cream Parlor!

"I can't explain it. It's surreal. I'm looking at a. . . ."

Suze Graham squinted her eyes "Jose? Can you still hear me? Jose?"

Silence.

"We seem to have lost connection with Jose Ruiz in Miami. We will work on getting him back as soon as we can. . . ."

Becky felt sorry for Suze Graham as she obviously struggled to maintain her composure. Becky had grown up watching Suze every evening. Her sparkling green eyes almost imperceptibly darted back and forth as she cheerfully read reports of rising crime rates, wars, government upheavals, famine, diseases, economic collapses and the occasional surfing bull dog.

Now she stared out blankly from the television screen. Tears welled up in her eyes, and her voice quivered.

A studio man with large black headphones quietly slipped Suze a piece of paper. An odd expression crossed her face as she read the note. Her face turned pale as if she'd seen a ghost. She hesitated then spoke into the camera.

"We have just received an unconfirmed report. . .that New York City has been completely destroyed. Again this is unconfirmed. We are currently trying to establish communication with our sister station in New York City, and we will let you know the status of that situation just as soon as the information becomes available to us." Suze appeared to try hard to remain calm as she continued to deliver the news.

"A spokesman for the North American Union has said that emergency aid centers are being set up all along the Eastern seaboard. Survivors are being cared for, and search-and-rescue operations are currently underway in many locations."

As Suze read from the overhead monitor, shaky video of frightened victims flickered across the television screen. Some were crying hysterically as they searched for their lost loved ones through rows of the dead covered with white sheets waiting to be identified and claimed.

A wall covered with photographs and desperately scrawled notes came into view. The camera zoomed in on a picture of a smiling man sitting at a table with a birthday cake and candles caught on film in mid-snap. The photo was stuck to the wall with masking tape. Becky could barely read the uneven handwriting underneath: "Have you seen our dad? Brad Williams. AGE: 42. EYES: Brown. HAIR: Brown. 5'11", 185 lbs. Please call Nicole: (305) 555-7645."

The camera pulled back and panned along the wall revealing several homemade fliers, frantically plastered on top of one another.

"Relief organizations are bracing for unprecedented demands. The Red Cross just released a statement saying that the lack of drinking water, food and shelter will be their number one concern in the aftermath of this disaster. The World Union has pledged more than three hundred million Ameros in aid so far." Suze's feminine voice sounded dismal.

She continued. "Scientists have just confirmed there was an eruption of the Cumbre Vieja Volcano in the Canary Islands off the coast of Western Africa. Reports indicate the western flank of the mountain collapsed in the ocean, triggering the devastating five-hundred-foot waves which wreaked havoc throughout the Atlantic Ocean."

"Unbelievable!" Momma shook her head. It was the first word anyone had said in nearly an hour.

"More breaking news now: In response to concerns of looting, the president has announced martial law

throughout the North American Union beginning immediately. Also, the World Union Food Program will review
food supplies and adjust rations to compensate for the
losses caused by the disaster. We can expect 'per-
household' rations to be lowered in the coming days. The
president reminds citizens that hoarding food is punishable by up to ten years in prison."

"All those poor people," Momma said as she hit the
mute button on the remote control. Suze Graham's voice
went silent, and closed captioning began to scroll beneath
her bewildered stare. "I'm going to call the hospital. I'm
sure we'll be involved in the rescue efforts in some way."
Momma stood and walked to the kitchen, David in tow.

Becky wasn't listening; she was deep in her own
thoughts. She heard her mother mumble something about
the poor tsunami victims and how she wished she could
help.

The news footage of the people searching through
the rows of dead bodies sent a searing pain through her
heart. She couldn't erase from her mind the lady screaming
hysterically as she recognized her child's motionless body
lying under the sheet.

Her father's words interrupted her thoughts. "This
is all we needed." He sighed. "As if the economy wasn't bad
enough already, there is no way the World Union can deal
with something like this. Do you realize what it will cost to
rebuild?" His voice climbed to a low roar. Becky could feel
one of her father's tirades coming on. He often vented his
frustrations with forces greater than himself through long,
impassioned monologues in which he outlined all that the
government had done wrong in the past twenty years.

Video continued to glow silently from the television.
Suze Graham's voice crept along the bottom of the screen
in the form of misspelled captions. A timestamp in the
corner indicated the pictures had been shot earlier in the
day. Becky's chest tightened as she watched a young,

14

blond-haired woman clutch a lifeless toddler to her breast and rock back and forth in agony.

Sadness, fear and then anger swept over her. *If there is a God—how could he allow this to happen? Why did he let so many innocent people die?*

The images were unbearable. Becky realized the living room was now dark. Night had sneaked into the house while their attention was fixed on the pictures beamed to them from the east side of the union. She was depressed and wanted to be alone. She stood and left her father sitting on the couch staring blankly at the glowing screen. She brushed away a tear that had escaped her watery eyes as she climbed up the dark hardwood stairs to her bedroom. Becky closed the door quietly behind her. She sneered at the fresh coats of rosy pink paint she had picked out only a year ago. She and Momma had an awful fight over her choice of colors. The terrible words she had said to her momma echoed through her memory as she pulled her stuffed brown rabbit with its big blue bow from the top of her white bookcase. Blake Collins's muscles rippled beneath his football uniform as he smiled charmingly at her from the poster hung over her twin bed.

Hugging the soft animal, she lay on her bed and stared up as red-and-blue lights of a passing police car strobed across her ceiling. A flash of fear vibrated through her body as she instantly recalled the night of the big earthquake when her father was injured and so many people had died.

When she closed her eyes she could easily return to that terrifying morning: climbing over toppled furniture and broken glass, her home—everything that was ever familiar and comforting to her—suddenly unrecognizable.

First it was the earthquake and now this terrible tsunami. Why do so many people have to die?

She shook her head involuntarily as the image of the young, blond woman rocking her dead toddler flashed before her again. She fought back tears as those same desperate feelings resurged in her throat.

Why is this happening?

The stuffed rabbit rolled to its side as she released it and stood up. She crossed over to her desk and sat down at the white wooden chair in front of her computer monitor and flicked on the metal switch.

"Good evening, Rebekah!" a young sexy male voice said from the speakers. "Please enter your password."

She quickly typed "busterkitty" on the keyboard and waited. Soon a smiling Blake Collins clutching a football posing for the cover of *Aquarius Sports* magazine appeared on the screen.

Becky clicked on the icon that took her to her favorite search engine and then typed a series of words: tsunami, disaster, end of the world, apocalypse, prophecy, and who is God? She randomly clicked on a few of the thousands of websites and blogs and even watched a couple of videos. Each had its own theory as to what had caused the recent disasters. And each was absolutely sure they were right and everyone else was wrong. Some blamed global warming while others warned it was the "end of the world."

Loud rapping on her bedroom door startled her.

"BECKY!" yelled her brother. He was the spitting image of their father, with his brown hair and brown eyes. His young voice grated on her nerves. "T.J. IS ON THE PHONE!"

"I'm busy. Tell her I'll see her at school tomorrow."

"BECKY!" he persisted. "T.J.'S ON THE PHONE. SHE WANTS TO TALK TO YOU ABOUT CHEERLEADING PRACTICE."

Becky couldn't tell if her little brother was honestly communicating her friend's urgent message or simply delighting in annoying her. "Go away and leave me alone!" she said calmly but loudly without taking her eyes off her computer monitor.

"BECKY." He continued pounding. "BECKY. . . BECKY! YOU'D BETTER ANSWER ME! MOMMA SAID THERE IS NO SCHOOL TOMORROW!"

"Then just tell T.J. I will call her back later."

Becky's brain tried to tune him out. *Hmm. I wonder why there's no school tomorrow? Maybe it has something to do with that martial law thing.*

She sighed when the pounding stopped and she heard the sound of padded footsteps running down the hardwood stairs.

She continued to focus on the information that glowed from her monitor. She found many Bible verses quoted in the blog entries she'd read. The words sounded tantalizingly foreign. As she read the lines with mounting curiosity they began to fit together like clues in an ancient riddle. She urgently clicked on one link after another, following the verses deeper into the blogs and the endless theories of signs missed, prophecies forgotten and warnings of what was to come. They appeared on her screen in fragments: frustrating bits and pieces of a grand story like previews of the summer blockbusters at the movie theater.

Finally Becky clicked onto a link that took her to an online bookstore. She typed in her shipping address and used Momma's credit card number to purchase a book.

Knowing she would face an inquisition when the credit card statement arrived, Becky volunteered that she had bought a book online. "Just a book I needed for school."

■■

A week later Becky found the brown paper package in the mailbox with her name on it. She eagerly waited until after dinner to lock herself in her room away from her family's prying eyes and the incessant news of the disaster on the East Coast blaring nonstop on the living room television.

She hurried over to the nightstand next to her bed. Her fingers clicked on the pink lamp illuminating various shades of mauve all around her room.

She pulled open the top drawer and found the package she had stashed away earlier that afternoon out of Momma's sight. She used her fingernails to break the brown packing tape at the edges and easily pried open the flimsy cardboard box to reveal a book bound in black leather. The gold lettering glistened under her pink lamp: *Holy Bible*.

She plopped onto her tummy on her neatly made bed and stuffed a pillow under her chest. She fingered through the thin, delicate pages edged with gold. With every turn the crisp paper crackled like a shotgun blast in the soft, pink quiet of her room. The smell of the new leather reminded her of her grandfather.

Slowly she thumbed the pages, felt her lips form the sounds of the ancient words printed in bold black ink: Genesis, Exodus, Leviticus, Numbers, Deuteronomy. She knew these names. They were the same as the names in her father's book, the Jewish Tanakh.

She flipped to the back of the Bible: Matthew, Mark, Luke, John. She paused and began to read the small, dense text in the book of John.

"In the beginning was the Word, and the Word was with God, and the Word was God; the same was in the beginning with God" (John 1:1-2).

"And the Word was made flesh, and dwelt among us, and we beheld his glory, the glory as of the only begotten of the Father, full of grace and truth" (John 1:14).

Her eyes scanned the pages while her mind grasped the information.

"For God so loved the world that he gave his only begotten Son, that whosoever believeth in him should not perish, but have everlasting life" (John 3:16).

"And we believe and are sure that thou art that Christ, the Son of the living God" (John 6:69).

18

She turned the crisp white pages back to Matthew 24.

"For nation shall rise against nation, and kingdom against kingdom: and there shall be famines, and pestilences, and earthquakes, in divers places. All these are the beginning of sorrows" (Matthew 24:7-8).

The beginning of sorrows? Again the image of the mother rocking her dead child flashed before her eyes. *Maybe we are in the beginning of sorrows?*

Becky didn't read in any particular order. She read a chapter for a while, and then she skipped to another book. She tried to store all the scriptures and footnotes in her head. She strained her eyes as she read into the wee hours of the morning. Her heavy eyes finally succumbed, and she fell into a deep sleep. A series of images, thoughts and emotions traveled through her mind. . . .

■■■

Wearing red shorts and a white T-shirt, Becky flung the bulging white garbage bag over the fence. She listened as it landed with a clink and a thud in the overflowing dumpster concealed on the other side. Becky knitted her brow in disgust and grumbled quietly to herself. "Why does David never get told to take out the trash?"

The mid-morning sun parted the hazy, blue sky as she walked along the wide service road that separated a community park from her cluttered, walled-in backyard. The moist chill of night still hung in the air, but the warm sun on her bare legs told her she could expect a typical, comfortable Southern California spring day.

She thought of small projects that could help her pass the long, quiet hours that stretched out before her. School had been cancelled again—more shortages caused by the disaster on the East Coast.

Her muscles rebelled at the idea of practicing her cheerleading routine again. She had filled the previous day with hours of jumping and tumbling in her backyard.

She noticed people gathered around a large, white tent that had been erected near the baseball diamond.

Wednesday mornings were not the usual time for weddings or graduation celebrations to overtake the park and clog the few precious parking spaces in the neighborhood.

Her head burned with curiosity. She bounded down the small embankment, her flip-flops stained black with use, through overgrown weeds and onto the baseball field.

White rope and aluminum poles held up the heavy canvas that flapped in lazy protest against a soft breeze.

A short, plump lady stood outside the tent. She dabbed her eyes with tissue absorbing the tears streaming down her round, rosy cheeks.

Cautiously Becky approached the entrance. The bright morning sun was diluted to a dirty, yellow light as it poured through the canvas.

People were crowded near the center, gravitating toward a man robed in white. A long, unkempt black beard concealed the lower half of his face while a neatly wrapped turban covered a large cranial bump on the top of his head. He stood like a giant with his eyes closed, seemingly oblivious that the crowd focused intensely on him.

Becky looked around her. No one had noticed her. She slowly stepped inside and stood with her back against one of the aluminum poles.

A young boy kneeled before the bearded man. Becky felt nervous anticipation fill the tent as the crowd stood in reverent silence. Like all the others gathered, she focused her attention on the bearded man. He reached out and grabbed both sides of the boy's head. A grimace washed over the bearded man's face as he clinched his eyes tight. Becky struggled to understand what she was watching. She thought of leaving, afraid she had intruded on something private. She quickly scanned the people in the crowd, hoping no one had noticed her.

She moved her foot as she prepared to exit. She would turn and walk, quickly, quietly and be back in the familiar surroundings of her home within minutes.

Before she could command her legs into motion, her eyes fixed on something she could not turn away from. As the bearded man's hands held the young, blond boy's head, his own body flung backward in a dramatic display of motion. The people gathered around him collectively gasped in a mixture of fear and awe. Becky noticed the dingy, yellow light coming through the canvas had become extremely bright and white.

Then her knees buckled beneath her as her mind tried to conceive of all she was seeing. The bearded man, his face still contorted, his hands still wrapped around the young boy's skull, began to lift off the ground. Slowly in his bare feet he stood on his toes and then completely left the floor.

Becky's mouth dropped open, and she stared wide eyed in disbelief. *OH, MY GOSH! THAT MAN IS FLOATING IN THIN AIR!*

His body became elongated as he silently rose. The gold silk scarf tied neatly around his waist hung loosely. The young boy stood up from his kneeling position as the bearded man's arms stretched to maintain his grip on the boy's head. The bearded man hovered about two feet off the ground.

Becky's heart pounded wildly. She became aware that her mouth was hanging wide open. The people gathered around him knelt and stared adoringly, waiting, building to an expected crescendo.

"YOU ARE HEALED!" The bearded man's voice exploded like a loudspeaker through the thick canvas walls and echoed throughout the park. He released the boy with a flamboyant gesture. A woman who had been standing near the boy looked quizzically at the child. A low murmur of voices moved through the crowd.

The boy turned to the woman and smiled. "Mother, I can hear!"

"Johnny?!" The woman's voice cracked with tears as she bent down and embraced her son. "It is a miracle!"

A shock of energy moved through the tent, and the people suddenly contracted closer to the bearded man. The woman looked up at him, fighting to control her sobs of joy "Thank you, Jesus. Thank you! Thank you, Jesus!" Still clutching the boy to her chest she fell to her knees. With one hand she reached for the hem of the bearded man's robe and sobbed.

Others in the crowd began to weep. "JESUS! JESUS!" the people began to chant in unison. "PRAISE YE THE MESSIAH!"

Becky remembered the scenes of miracles she had read in her Bible. *Was this what it was like for those who witnessed the work of Jesus of Nazareth?*

She could not deny the hope that had leapt through her mind or the overwhelming excitement that pulsated through the tent.

Could it really be? She wrung her hands together as she watched the people reach for the bearded man, tears streaming down their faces, struggling against each other to touch him.

She felt her own eyes moisten with tears. *Had he seen the tragedy on the East Coast? Had he seen the mother rocking her dead toddler in her arms? Had he heard her cry out in anguish? Had he come to save us?*

She pulled herself away from the scene in the tent and hurried back through the weeds to her home.

She could still hear faint, jubilant chants of "PRAISE JESUS" and "HALLELUJAH" as she clicked the sliding glass door shut behind her.

David sat on the couch in the living room, a bowl of popcorn on his lap. He didn't acknowledge her when she entered the room. His eyes were on the line of survivors stretching through the rubble-strewn streets of Miami. Suze Graham's tired voice pleaded with viewers to donate as much food, clothing and money as they could.

The desperation on the faces on the television was completely incongruous with the hope and happiness she had brought with her from the tent in the park.

"David," she said as she plopped herself heavily down onto the couch cushion next to him in a deliberate effort to break his attention away from the television.

"What?" He begrudgingly acknowledged her presence.

Becky exhaled a long breath, uncertain of how to broach a subject she wasn't even sure she wanted to discuss with her little brother.

"What?" David said impatiently again.

"Do you think Jesus would come to us? Here? Now?" Her voice was halting. She didn't look at David. Instead she focused on the scenes of devastation flashing on the television. Exhaustion stung the face of a white-haired black man in tattered clothes as he pushed an overweight woman through knee-deep sand and mud in a shopping cart.

Becky felt her brother's eyes on her. She swallowed nervously.

"What are you talking about?" he asked as he munched on a white puffed-out kernel.

"There is so much pain in the world. With the wars, the earthquake and now the tsunami, don't you think Jesus would want to do something? Don't you think he'd try to help, if even just a little?" Becky continued to stare at the television.

"What the heck has gotten you on this?" David was genuinely curious.

"There is some kind of revival or something going on in the park. I know it's crazy. . . ." She searched her mind for the right words to describe what she had seen.

23

"This man did stuff. Amazing stuff! There were no wires or smoke and mirrors or anything. And if you had seen how people reacted. . . . He really had an effect. I could feel it."

David's brow arched. Becky knew his look of sarcasm. "Becky, that magician made the entire Statue of Unity disappear. Was he Jesus too?"

Becky felt a twinge of embarrassment at her younger brother's stoic skepticism.

"'For as lightning comes from the East and flashes to the West, so shall the coming of the son of man be,'" he continued.

"What?" Becky was surprised to hear David quote Scripture.

"'If they say to you, "Look, he is in the desert!" do not go out; or "Look, he is in the inner rooms!" do not believe it!'"

"You're right," Becky conceded. "I mean, I didn't really think. . .it was just nice to think there was someone who could fix things."

Becky stood and left her brother on the couch.

Her curiosity led her back down the hill and through the field to where the crowd of people and the bearded floating man were still gathered beneath the tent. Again she stood unnoticed near the entrance as people shouted, "PRAISE JESUS!" Again Becky felt joy wrap around her. The energy of the tent was addictive.

She stared at the bearded man; his bare feet were planted back on the ground. She became aware of a longing to touch him. She wanted to reach out, like all those crowded around him, and touch his robes. Her legs began moving her toward the white light that seemed to radiate from him.

"Come, my child." The voice was muted, as if it was audible only in her own head. It was the bearded man. His deep, brown eyes locked with hers. "Come," he said again, softly in a deep mesmerizing tone.

24

All those who had been pressing close to him and praising him now backed away and cleared a path between Becky and the bearded man. They stared at her. Becky relived her fear standing before the judges at cheerleading tryouts.

"It's okay, dear." A lady's voice prodded her forward. "He's here to save us. Let him save you too, child."

Becky's flip-flop dangled as she slowly moved her foot forward. Her instincts screamed at her to turn and run, but she could not turn away from the bearded man. His gaze held her tight. She realized she was walking forward, closing the gap between them. As she neared him, she felt warmth cover her body as if she were sinking into a hot bath.

She stopped and looked up into his deep, black, radiant eyes.

His thick eyebrows pulled together as he smiled and examined her face.

A strange power was there that held Becky both fascinated and yet afraid. Her skin began to crawl with an indefinable sense of unease.

The bearded man leaned over her. She felt a cold, bony finger stroke her cheek.

"What is your name, my child?" he asked.

Becky remembered her brother's sarcastically arched brow, and she felt an arctic chill run down her spine.

She slowly inhaled the tent air into her lungs then blurted, "Jesus would know my name!"

The bearded man's thin lips tightened into a sneer, and his dark eyes locked into a frozen stare as if he was ready to devour his prey.

A sudden coldness hit Becky in the pit of her belly. Her body began to shake involuntarily with quick, short movements. She took a step backward.

The woman whose son was healed stared angrily at her and said, "How dare you mock Jesus!"

Becky could feel the people closing in around her, caging her like an animal. Her breath became panicked.

"Who are you to deny our lord?" someone from the crowd shouted, their words enraged.

A surge of adrenaline shot through Becky's veins. She pushed through the crowd, knocking an older man to the ground. "GET AWAY FROM ME!" she screamed as she pushed. "WHAT DO YOU WANT?" Cold hands grabbed at her arms and shoulders and legs. "LEAVE ME ALONE!"

She saw the inviting bright sunlight streaming through the tent opening and bounded toward it. A hand grabbed her lower leg. She tried to kick it free. It was pulling her back into the tent. . . .

Her eyes suddenly jarred opened. Her red-and-green plastic hummingbird nightlight cast long, faded shadows against the walls. She was safe in her room, in her bed and not in that horrible tent in the park anymore. She held her pillow in a death grip. Her heart and breath mimicked each other. Moisture gathered on the back of her neck like condensation on a glass of iced tea. She looked at the clock on her nightstand, 4:34 A.M.

Her breathing began to calm. She closed her eyes and replayed the dream in her mind over and over again.

She tried to figure out what she had just seen and felt. The quiet of the wee hours fueled her thoughts. *How was David able to quote Scripture verses from the Bible?* she wondered. *Maybe this dream was a message—or maybe a warning from God?*

Her body tingled, and her muscles were still tightened, alert and ready for a fight. She rolled over in her bed and looked at her new Bible resting on the nightstand. The gold lettering shimmered even in the low light.

"Dear Jesus," she whispered softly. "I believe[5] you are the Christ, the Son of the living God. I believe in you, and I want to be belong to you. Amen."

She closed her eyes. The stillness of the night enveloped her. She felt herself relax and her mind quiet. She drifted off into a peaceful slumber. . . .

And then shall appear the sign of the Son of man in heaven: and then shall all the tribes of the earth mourn, and they shall see the Son of man coming in the clouds of heaven with power and great glory. And he shall send his angels with a great sound of a trumpet, and they shall gather together his elect from the four winds, from one end of heaven to the other.
Matthew 24:30-31

---

[5] "That if thou shalt confess with thy mouth the Lord Jesus, and shalt believe in thine heart that God hath raised him from the dead, thou shalt be saved" (Romans 10:9).

SCARS

2

THE DAY OF PENTECOST

"Hap-py Pen-te-cost!" the guard speaks in broken English with a rare smile as he retrieves the breakfast tray.

Becky forces a smile and nods as he walks away from her door and disappears into the dark corridor. His cheerful whistle echoes off the block walls. She recognizes the tune as the old Christmas carol, "God Rest Ye, Merry Gentlemen," but she knows that isn't the song he whistles to himself. Instead he's whistling the new version rewritten to praise the day Maitreyas emerged, the day now celebrated each year as the Pentecost.

Sounds of more singing and the clinking of glasses wash up from the unseen guard's break room at the end of the hall. Becky cannot help but scoff at their festivities. To Becky the Pentecost occurred more than two thousand years ago and held a vastly different meaning. She could never celebrate the day Maitreyas was revealed[6] to the world.

To Becky, the new Pentecost marked the beginning of the end. She has re-enacted that day and the events leading up to it in her head at least a million times. Every time she arrives at the same question, How could no one have known?

She closes her eyes and holds her hands over her ears trying to block the sound of the guard's off-tune singing. In her mind the hollow, foreign tunes meld into the cheers and joyful cries of thousands gathered in Saint Peter's Square on that day. She can see their tear-soaked, smiling faces looking up into the bright Roman sky in utter admiration. They are holding out their arms in devoted praise.

How could they not have known their cheers and songs were welcoming to the earth the first beast of Revelation?

■■

On an early August morning the world stood in tearful silence after the Vatican announced the pope's sudden death just as Maitreyas had predicted.

The media was in a frenzy—they all wanted an interview with Maitreyas. He was invited by WNN (World News Network) and the international media to speak directly to the entire world through the television networks all linked together by satellite.

He agreed to speak to the media at St. Peter's Square in Rome.

Months had passed since the tsunami had killed millions of people on the East Coast of the North American Union. The endless torrent of television coverage of the

---

[6] "Let no one deceive you by any means; for that Day will not come unless the falling away comes first, and the man of sin is revealed, the son of perdition" (2 Thessalonians 2:3).

disaster had slowed to only a few minutes dedicated at the beginning of each evening broadcast. Becky's school was back to a regular summer school session. And it had become a social norm to direct polite conversations away from the plight of the refugees to less depressing topics.

Momma had stopped relaying the experiences of the doctors from her work who had been dispatched to help with the recovery. Instead she indulged in conversations that centered on possible reasons for the neighbors' pending divorce.

Rations had been eased for those living in most major cities. And most people ignored criticism of the Film Stars' Association for holding their annual awards gala as scheduled.

Like most others, Becky had found it easy to divert her attention from the sad and discomforting images of families living in tents surrounded by festering piles of rubble. She sat with her back to the television, cradling the phone between her shoulder and ear and flipping the brightly colored pages of her teen magazine while she traded valuable bits of information about who-liked-whom with T.J. on the other end of the line.

It was during one of these comforting conversations with T.J. that Becky first learned of Maitreyas.

"I wish Maitreyas could tell me if Dennis is going to ask me to the dance," T.J. said plaintively.

"What? Who?" Becky asked when she heard the strange name.

"You know, Maitreyas. The man who can predict the future," T.J. explained.

"You mean that weird kid in geometry class who wears that long black coat?" Becky asked puzzled.

"Where have you been, girlfriend?" T.J. said with a tone of exasperation "It's all over the news. This guy in London, Maitreyas, he predicted the tsunami and the earthquake. They have proof of it. He's like a prophet or something."

"You mean like Nostradamus?" Becky said incredu-
lously.

"Kind of, but way more accurate. Seriously, he can,
like, talk to God or something."

There was a silence on the line as Becky pondered
the possibility.

"Really, girlfriend. You need to read the news once
in a while," T.J. admonished her.

Late that night Becky sat at her computer. Her room
was dark save for the blue light cast against her face by her
monitor as she scrolled through websites dedicated to the
teachings of Maitreyas.

She read in astonishment that *The London Times*
had quoted Maitreyas six weeks before the tsunami:

*"The greed of the West has placed the future of the
world in undeniable jeopardy. Because of their unwilling-
ness to change and share their resources with the rest of
the planet, a giant wall of seawater will hit the East Coast
of the Americas causing great death and destruction. . . ."*

In the quiet of the late night she clicked on one link
after another. Thousands of pages and headlines reported
on the story of Maitreyas and his teachings.

"BRIGHT STAR HERALDS MAITREYAS'S EMERGENCE"

*"Our great world teacher, Maitreyas, traces his
ancestry to the ancient tribe of Dan in the Holy Land,"*
one website quoted.

*"Like the Buddha, Maitreyas is a fully self-
actualized, enlightened being. He brings hope and peace
to us."*

Becky's eyes darted back and forth across her monitor as she quickly absorbed the information and clicked on the next page.

"Maitreyas shares his peace and wisdom with us. He warns that mankind's greed and arrogance threaten God's greatest gift, our planet and all its abundance. He teaches us to heed the warning signs: melting glaciers, hurricanes and rising temperatures. In his wisdom, Maitreyas counsels us to practice the 'principle of sharing.' The wealthy nations of the world must provide for the poor. Only through the 'principle of sharing' can humankind avoid complete destruction."

At the bottom of the page a link to a World Union Network story jumped to Becky's attention. She clicked and read the headline dated three weeks ago:

"WORLD LEADERS LISTEN CLOSELY TO MAITREYAS."

The bold words spread across the monitor beneath a constantly spinning WNN logo.

"Unable to deny the uncanny accuracy of his predictions about the great Hollywood quake a few years ago and the recent East Coast tsunami disaster, more and more world leaders are turning to the teacher Maitreyas for advice on everything from foreign and economic policy to the best times for scheduling meetings."

On the sidebar Becky found a list of more recent articles about Maitreyas. She clicked on the headline:

"LATEST PREDICTION FROM MAITREYAS SENDS SHOCKWAVE THROUGH WORLD HEADQUARTERS."

"In the wake of his accurate predictions of two major world disasters, world leaders scramble to make sense of Maitreyas's latest prediction which he made to followers earlier this week. He told a stunned audience, 'In the eighth month of this year, the "Glory of the Olive" shall be cut off in the city of seven hills, and in the final persecution of the Holy Roman Church, there will reign Petrus Romanus[7] who will feed his flock amid many tribulations. . . .'"

Becky scratched her head trying to make sense of the riddle. "If the president doesn't know what it means then I certainly don't have a chance of understanding it," she whispered to herself.

■■

The words of Maitreyas took on clear significance on August 11. Becky and her brother sat in the air-conditioned living room and watched in solemn silence as crowds of mourners stood in pouring rain at St. Peter's Square.

Suze Graham's voice spoke over the images. "His Holiness the pope was declared dead at 1:00 P.M. local time. Thousands of people, faithful and non-faithful alike, have crowded into St. Peter's Square to pay their respect to the man who strengthened the Catholic church through perilous times."

---

[7]   The last pope as prophesied by St. Malachy is "Peter the Roman," whose pontificate will end in the destruction of the city of Rome. 1590. (Cucherat, "Proph. de la succession des papes," ch. xv).

Becky imagined her mother, who was at work, whispering a prayer and crossing herself when she heard the news that her pope had died.

Suze Graham's voice continued. "It has become clear that this is the event Maitreyas predicted two months ago. With the death of the pope the 'glory of the olive' has been cut off from the 'city of the seven hills,' which, of course, refers to the city of Rome. Many are now wondering when the rest of the prediction will be realized. Who is Petrus Romanus?"

In the weeks that followed, Becky could no longer remember a time when she did not know of Maitreyas. His name was everywhere; on the radio and television, in newspapers and on the internet. Life slowed as people waited anxiously for his next move. Weddings were postponed, trading in the world markets virtually stopped, parliaments put their debates on hold and homebuyers stalled in signing their mortgages as everyone knew that Maitreyas and his revelation of the mysterious Petrus Romanus could forever change the destiny of all mankind.

On a dull, cool evening in November, two days before Grandma Silver succumbed to the flu pandemic, Becky sat at the dining room table leaning back in a dark-cherry wood chair, her feet propped up on the table with her pink phone plastered to her ear chatting with T.J.

The clanging sounds of pots and pans rang from the kitchen as Momma slammed the doors of the solid white cabinets and wiped clean the black granite counters and shiny stainless steel appliances. She busily rinsed leftover spaghetti noodles down the drain and put the dishes in the dishwasher.

In the family room in his big brown leather recliner watching the sports channel, Dad sat comfortably in his Levis and white T-shirt, slightly stained by a drop of spaghetti sauce, while David sat cross-legged on the family room floor, his elbows resting on his knees and his chin cupped in his hands. A blue-and-red space helmet headset fit snuggly to his skull as he played "Timmy Time Traveler," a virtual reality game played by using your mind.

Dad's football game was interrupted by an alarming buzz that screamed from the television and shattered the evening's domestic tranquility. Becky recognized the noise as the emergency notification system that had become so familiar in recent years. The alarm would be followed by the announcement of another quake, flood or war, or perhaps the pandemic had claimed more lives in the heartland of the North American Union.

"We interrupt this program to bring you the following special announcement." Suze Graham appeared on the screen, a flush of excitement in her cheeks.

"Kirsten! Come in here quick! It's on!" Dad yelled. The recliner squeaked beneath his weight.

"Rebekah! Get off the telephone!"

Momma rushed into the living room, wiping her wet hands on her tan cotton shorts as she sat down on the faded leather couch next to Dad's recliner. David yanked off the headset and flung it aside. Becky hurried through the arched doorway and sat down on the couch next to her mother. She laughed out loud when she noticed David's brown hair sticking up all over his head from the headset. The Silvers had assembled around the forty-six-inch LCD TV.

"We now go live to St. Peter's Square in Rome. . . ." Suze's voice was excited. Becky gasped at the image on the screen. A picture from high above the ancient city of seven hills showed a sea of people molded in the familiar shape of St. Peter's Square. The great crowd spilled out of the square and into the contorting, narrow streets between the red-tiled houses surrounding the great basilica.

"Thank you, Suze," a female reporter's voice said over the remarkable images. "We are live here in Vatican

City where millions of people have gathered from all over the world expecting to hear Maitreyas speak.

"You are looking at pictures from our helicopter above Rome as people continue to stream into the city in unprecedented numbers. The European Union's government has been working to accommodate these crowds. For the past five days millions of people have arrived in Rome by train, plane, bus. Many even walked here from as far away as Paris. On the outskirts of the city the highways leading to Rome are filled with people trying to make their way here to the Vatican. And everyone is here for one reason. Everyone wants to know what Maitreyas will voice next."

The picture on the television changed from the aerial view of Rome to a tight shot of the pretty reporter. She brushed her long, jet-black hair neatly to one side with one hand as she held her microphone close to her lips with the other. "Since the Vatican announced that Maitreyas would address the world here on the steps of one of Christianity's most famous landmarks, many have speculated about what he would say."

The camera pulled back to reveal a young, unkempt man standing next to the reporter. "This is Trevor Sutton, who came here all the way from Bristol, England." The young man smiled at the camera. "What do you hope to hear Maitreyas say today, Trevor?"

The young man spoke deliberately into the microphone. "I think he will make another prediction about the future. I hope he will tell us how we can avoid another disaster like the tsunami so we can save many lives."

The reporter moved the microphone back toward her own face. "I've heard a lot of people here theorize that Maitreyas is an alien from another world. Some have even suggested a wild conspiracy theory that he is part of the Reptilian race and that they created humans. Do you believe any of those ideas?"

"Who knows?" The young man shrugged, looking at the camera. "Nobody can explain how he can predict the future, so anything is possible. All I know is that he has great powers and the world needs someone like him now, to lead us and help us." The man's smile faded, and he looked at the reporter. His voice quivered. "That's why I came here. The idea that the world will continue on this way—so much violence, despair, hatred—it's unbearable. Maitreyas can change all of that. He will change it. He has to."

"Thank you." The reporter turned from the young man and spoke to the camera. "As you can see, Suze, there is a lot of hope here. Hundreds of thousands of people have gathered in this ancient square, between these famous, massive colonnades representing the outstretched arms of the Catholic church, hoping to hear Maitreyas deliver a very important message of hope to the world."

A stir of excitement in the crowd alerted the reporter that activity was taking place on a stage erected at the entrance to the great basilica. The televised image switched to a live video feed shared by all the worldwide networks covering the story. Becky's father clicked the remote, flipping quickly between channels, confirming that everyone was airing the same image.

A cardinal bishop stood behind a speaker's podium filled with microphones. Behind the cardinal, stone reliefs of the saints and angels seemed to dance across the façade of the towering church as the warm glow of the Italian afternoon stretched ancient shadows over the stage. The cardinal was clad in the traditional ruby-red vestment with a scarlet ferraiolo draped over his shoulders and tied underneath his neck.

His sparkly eyes peered through thick wire-rimmed glasses.

As the cameraman worked to establish a shot, his shaky movements revealed a powerfully made man standing behind the cardinal, in the shadows of the basilica. The man was more than six feet tall with broad shoulders. He wore a white-washed robe that hung close to his muscular physique and brushed the ground around his sandal-clad feet. A purple silk cape was tied loosely around his neck and draped down his strong back.

Becky gazed at the screen. *I wonder if that man is Maitreyas?*

She closed her eyes momentarily and prayed silently. *Dear Jesus, please protect me and shield me from anything that may harm me coming through the television. In Jesus' name, amen.*

The cardinal began to speak. His singsong Italian vibrated from large speakers standing to either side of the stage. His voice redoubled itself off the marble columns and bounced down the narrow, marble and concrete canyons of the old imperial city.

"*Fratelli, grazie per aver veniti qui. . . .*"

The television whispered softly in English, interpreting the cardinal's Italian for the American audience. "Thank you for coming, brothers and sisters."

"*Oggi e' il giorno che noi abbiamo aspetato per tanto tempo.*"

"Today is the day we have all been waiting for!"

Most of the cardinal's hair was gone, and he hunched slightly forward as he spoke carefully into the mass of microphones before him. Bright rays of sunlight danced off the large, ornate gold cross that hung on his chest.

"*E' un gran piacere ed onore a presentarvi. . . .*"

"It gives me great honor and privilege to introduce to you"—the voice of the interpreter paused as the cardinal hesitated, as if he had just become aware of the weight of the event and worried his words would not measure up—

"*Vi do, Petrus Romanus!*"

"I give you Peter Roma!"

The cardinal turned with a grand flourish and flung his arm wide, extending his hand to the tall man standing behind him. Peter Roma walked slowly forward out of the shadows and into the bright sunlight.

A roar erupted from the crowd and out through the speakers, filling the living room and rattling Becky's and David's school portraits that hung delicately on the wall behind the television. Becky's father quickly fingered the remote and lowered the volume.

The camera pulled back to a wide shot of the square to capture visually the excitement viewers were already witnessing through audio.

The ocean of people covering the square bubbled and swelled with glee. The flags of the unions waved majestically back and forth over the crowd, their arms lifted high in praise, throwing hats into the air in joyful abandon.

The din rose out of the square and drifted over the city like a cloud. The cardinal stepped aside and sat down in an empty chair in the shade cast by the church.

Peter Roma stood behind the microphones, his dove-white robe fluttering elegantly in the breeze. His black wavy hair framed his long thin face. A distinguished beard rested on his strong jawline and outlined his full lips.

The camera zoomed in tight, and Peter Roma's beautiful face filled the television screen. Becky thought he looked oddly familiar. He reminded her of a painting she had seen hanging in Momma's church. Then she thought of the shroud of Turin she had seen in a television documentary and the regal, serene face mysteriously imprinted on those ancient linens. As Peter Roma stared into the camera his face seemed to mimic the cloth. He was beautiful, but like the shroud something was missing. He was not a complete picture. And the mystery of what one could not see was powerful.

Becky saw strength and wisdom in his sturdy brow, kindness and humility etched into the delicate lines framing his eyes. His intense eyes stared into the camera in

St. Peter's Square and out from the television into Becky's living room and held her as if he had wrapped his powerful arms around her. Becky stared back into his eyes through the television screen and felt sadness. It was like looking down a deep well and seeing the pain of all humanity reflected up from the dark, glassy waters below.

Becky broke away from Peter Roma's hypnotic gaze and looked over at her mother. Her eyes did not blink as she stared into the glow of the television.

"Greetings," the male interpreter said in English over Peter Roma's strong masculine voice.

"I come to you in love."

St. Peter's Square fell into still silence as Peter Roma's gentle yet powerful voice rolled over the crowd, through the colonnades and into the streets of Rome.

"What is love? Love is a mystery—the greatest mystery of the universe. Love is your true inner self—self-realization that comes from God. It is the fountain of truth. Love is an energy that existed before anything was. This planet was created with love. . . ."

The camera zoomed in on twelve resplendent Swiss guardsmen standing at attention, six on each side of the entrance to the basilica. Bright blue-and-yellow bands of material covered their red doublets and breeches set off by a thick white collar enveloping their necks. A black helmet topped with red ostrich feathers balanced on their heads while one white-gloved hand grasped the halberd, its ax blade and pick with a spearhead on top, glistening in the sun.

"As some of you may be aware, we are entering into the New Age, the golden age of Aquarius—an age of splendor and of light! This new age ushers in a new revelation, and with this new revelation comes a new world teacher. This new revelation will be based on all the past and present world religions and will consist of a *new* approach to God. Over the past 2,800 years many teachers provided the world with a spiritual knowledge for mankind. Three of the greatest teachers were Muhammad, the Buddha, and Jesus of Nazareth."

A smile formed on his lips revealing perfect straight ivory teeth.

"Jesus of Nazareth came in love, and because of his love he gave over his body to be crucified."

He folded his hands together and looked straight into the camera. He stared for a moment then continued, "I am he. . . ."

Becky shook her head, certain she had misunderstood. She leaned into the television and furrowed her brow in an effort to listen as closely as she could.

"I am Jesus of Nazareth. I was crucified more than two thousand years ago."

"Huh?" Becky's jaw dropped. A frigid chill worked its way up the back of her spine while goose bumps blanketed her arms and legs.

The picture on the television switched to a shot of the crowd. The camera zoomed in on a woman with tears streaking her cheeks. She fingered the sign of the cross over her chest and lipped, "Father, Son, Holy Spirit, amen."

A man nearby shook his head in disbelief and gave a mocking smile in the direction of the podium.

"Is that really Jesus, Mommy?" David's eyebrows lifted high over his brown eyes.

"Shush!" Momma frowned, putting her finger to her lips.

The camera focused back on Peter Roma. The orange afternoon sun bathed the grey stones of the great basilica in a lukewarm glow, offering an uneasy backdrop as Peter Roma continued speaking.

"I was known by many names. I was Joshua the son of Nun. I was Isaiah. After Jesus of Nazareth, I was Apollonius of Tyana. I am now an ascended master. I am Isa as foretold by the prophet Muhammad, and in my last and final incarnation I am 'Petrus Romanus, the master of wisdom'!"

Becky felt her stomach tighten into one big knot.

"Please do not be confused. I am not 'the Christ.' 'The Christ' and I are two separate individuals. As Jesus of Nazareth, I channeled the power of 'the Christ' to survive my death and resurrection. It was 'the Christ's' power, not mine."[8]

He lifted his hands and held them to the camera.

"I do not have any scars from my death and resurrection for I have ascended with a new body. . . ."

Becky glanced down at her own hands, smooth and soft. She imagined the blinding pain of a hard, metal nail driving through the flesh. *Christ's wounds were more than mere scars,* she thought. *They symbolized a bond, a promise, above all, a sacrifice of immeasurable proportions.*

She looked at the large, smooth, soft hands Peter Roma proudly displayed to the world. *Would Jesus erase the symbols of his sacrifice, his love?* she asked herself.

Her blood simmered inside her at Peter Roma's suggestion of such callous vanity in her Savior. "Peter Roma is an imposter!" she wanted to scream at the television. "He has no scars because he is a fake and a liar! He is not Jesus of Nazareth, and he was never crucified! The real Jesus of Nazareth has scars—scars in his hands and on his feet from when he was nailed to the cross, and he has scars on his side from when he was struck by a spear. . . ."

Peter Roma lowered his hands to his sides.

"I have come to sit on St. Peter's seat, to lead the churches and guide mankind into the new age and to prepare the way for the Christ's return. As an ascended master it is my earthly duty to teach the 'love principle' and to rid the churches of their manmade dogmas which confuse the

---

[8]   "Who is a liar but he who denies that Jesus is the Christ? He is antichrist who denies both father and the son" (1 John 2:22).

43

minds of millions of people who otherwise would be ready for 'the Christ-the Logos of Eternal Love.'"

The camera zoomed to a small boy in a blue hooded jacket hunched over on his father's shoulders then back to Peter Roma.

"In this new age you must allow and invite God to speak to your conscious and join together with him and become one."

His piercing blue eyes looked over the crowd and focused on the red granite Egyptian obelisk, supported by bronze lions, standing watch over the square since the days of the emperors.

"As I have said before, this new age ushers in a new revelation, and with this new revelation comes a new world teacher. Using the 'love principle,' let us all open our hearts and our minds as I introduce you to the new world teacher, Bodhisattva, whose name in Sanskrit is derived from Maitra meaning 'universal love.' He will teach and guide mankind to a better, more loving and peaceful world."

Peter Roma extended his arm. "Please welcome 'Lord Maitreyas'!"

People's eyes searched the crowd trying to get a glimpse of Maitreyas. They were puzzled for no one came forward.

Again Peter Roma loudly announced, "The great teacher the world has been waiting for. . .'Lord Maitreyas.'"

In the shadowy recess of the entrance to the basilica, a flash of fluttering white caught the bright sunlight. A thin man stood framed by the massive bronze doors and the legions of stone saints and angels carved into the archways. His white robe moved gracefully in the warm breeze, and his turban glowed brilliantly in the dancing sun. An aura seemed to emanate from him as he emerged from the dark hollows of the basilica and onto the sunlit stage.

The bright glowing light was familiar to Becky.

"Oh, my gosh!" she blurted out loud, her voice shaky. "I've seen him before! He's the floating man from my dream!"

Momma, Dad and David paid no attention to Becky's astonishment. They continued staring quietly across the living room at the wide, flickering television screen.

With a narrow face and long sharp nose outlined by a coffee-black beard, Maitreyas held his chin up high as he approached the microphone-filled podium. The square was silent as the crowd curiously watched his movements.

Standing tall before the crowd and cameras, Maitreyas rolled his shoulders back and puffed out his broad chest. His elegant figure seemed to soar skyward like the great arches and dome of the basilica behind him. He closed his eyes then lifted both of his hands up toward heaven.

A roar like that of a thousand screaming jet engines erupted over the square. The sound of a strong gust of wind[9] descended on the crowd. People grabbed their hats as wind slapped at their faces and tousled their hair.

Shimmering waves of electromagnetic energy began to emanate from Maitreyas's body. His body glowed brightly in the fading afternoon light.

"Cool!" David bellowed.

Minutes passed as the crowd watched in stunned silence. Maitreyas slowly lowered his hands to his sides.

The roaring wind stopped, and the brilliant glow around Maitreyas's body faded.

Becky stared at the screen in disbelief. The television was silent. The crowds of thousands in the square stood still. Locked in place by a combination of fear and

---

[9] "When the Day of Pentecost had fully come. . .suddenly there came a sound from heaven, as of a rushing mighty wind. . .and began to speak with other tongues" (Acts 2:1-2, 4).

amazement, they were as quiet and motionless as the stone statues looking down on them from the top of the basilica.

"Imagine. . . ." Becky heard a deep, soothing voice speak. She looked around the living room. Her parents and David had not taken their eyes from the television screen. She turned her gaze back to the dark brown eyes of Maitreyas. They seemed to look directly at her through the television.

"Imagine. . . ."

She heard the voice again. Maitreyas's lips had not moved, but Becky knew the voice she heard was his. She looked at Momma, and by the deep creases in her forehead she knew she too had heard the voice. Becky looked back at the eyes staring out at her from the television.

"Imagine"—the gentle voice had a slight stutter as it echoed in her mind—"a world where there is no hunger and no suffering."

"Imagine. . .a world where goodwill overshadows the thoughts and hearts of all."

"Imagine. . .a world where there is no war, a world of peace[10] and goodwill."

His thick eyebrows curved above his dark amber eyes as he unblinkingly gazed into the camera.

Becky felt her heart twitch as it quickened. She turned her head in an effort to look away, but her eyes remained glued to Maitreyas's hypnotic gaze. She felt her muscles tense and an urge in her feet to start running. She remembered bright morning light shining through the entrance to the tent in her dream. She trembled with the same feeling of panic mixed with hopeful curiosity that held her at the feet of the bearded man who had come to her in her sleep.

"As Peter Roma has said, we have entered into a new age and a new revelation.

---

[10]   "And by peace shall destroy many" (Daniel 8:25).

"My beloveds, in this new age we can have a world of peace—because without peace there is no future. 'For broad is the road that leads to death and destruction, and many enter through it. But narrow is the road that leads to peace and unity.'

"My beloveds, humankind is on that wide road to death and destruction: Many are wealthy, greedy and wasteful while millions suffer and starve to death. There are economic crises, social unrest, division, starvation, environmental calamity and war. Humankind *must* change and take the narrow road that leads to unity, economic prosperity, happiness, environmental restoration and a golden era of peace and prosperity.

"The solution to get humankind back onto the right road is by sharing. You must start by sharing the world's food and resources. The resources of this world are given by divine right for *all* of humanity, not just the more privileged members of society. Food, housing, health care and education are *universal* rights for all.

"My beloveds, you must learn the 'principle of sharing,' and together we can feed the millions who are starving and suffer needlessly, and when you share you will recognize the love of God in yourselves. . . .

"You must make a choice. Either you continue on the wrong road and stay as you are—selfish, greedy, proud and self-destructive—or take the right road and accept me and my 'principle of sharing'—a path to peace and prosperity."

Maitreyas turned toward Peter Roma then back to the crowd of people.

"You have met my disciple Peter Roma. He was the earthly son of the blessed virgin Mary, queen of heaven, and is now the master of wisdom. He has ascended from the outer ray and is here to lead and guide all of the churches into this new age.

47

"You *must* put your trust in Peter Roma by allowing him the seat of St. Peter. By awakening the 'love principle,' he will guide the churches in this change."

He took a brief pause then continued to communicate without speaking.

"My beloveds. . .we are all *one.* You must accept that we are all *one,* and together we can transform our civilization into the most beautiful, peaceful civilization this world has never seen before. Together we can stop the planetary peril. Take the first step and let me lead you and show you the way. Allow me to help you and guide you so together we can create a brilliant new civilization where all may participate as equal members of humankind.

"Many of you will follow me and see me as their guide. Many will not.

"If you choose me and the 'principle of sharing,' the world will see peace and prosperity.

"If you reject me, death and destruction will continue to rain down upon the earth until it has destroyed itself. My beloveds, follow me. Accept me."

His lips formed a wry grin. His dark, glassy eyes continued staring forward. "Who am I, some of you may ask? I am that I am."

He raised his right hand in the air and made a sign. His third and fourth fingers were bent slightly forward. "Peace and goodwill to all."

He lowered his hand to his side then turned and walked back toward the entrance of the basilica. Peter Roma nodded as Maitreyas passed him.

The cardinal bishop lifted his hand and smiled and waved to the people, his solid gold ring reflecting the bright afternoon sun. He lowered his arm, and then he and Peter Roma turned and exited the stage. They moved past the colorful Swiss guardsmen and disappeared through the heavy, bronze doors of the basilica.

It was over.

The massive crowd began to move slowly. The flags and banners that had waved excitedly over their heads now bobbed listlessly above the bewildered masses, leading the way to the narrow, twisting streets of Rome and beyond, back to a world still in peril.

The pictures of the dispersing crowd beamed from helicopters high above the square abruptly changed to a closeup of the pretty, dark-haired news lady.

"Well, Suze, it appears as though the moment we all waited for has come and gone." She spoke breathlessly into the microphone held close to her lips. "Many people here in St. Peter's Square are not quite sure what they just saw and heard."

The video changed to a shot of Suze Graham sitting at her glass-and-steel desk in the WNN headquarters.

"Wow! That was powerful!" Suze said unscripted. "I'm not quite sure what I just saw and heard either!" Stray wisps of golden-blond hair drifted over her green eyes. "Did you see all that light coming off Lord Maitreyas's body?" she asked someone off camera. Then, remembering her professional obligation, she turned back to the camera and struggled to regain her composure.

"Our viewers should know we have spoken with our affiliates around the world. While we definitely heard Lord Maitreyas speaking—or communicating, I should say—in English, we are told by our affiliates in Japan that they heard him in Japanese, and the Russians heard him in Russian, and in Brazil they heard him in Portuguese." Suze Graham's voice quivered with amazement. She took a deep breath and deliberately slowed the pace of her speech.

"We are receiving calls and e-mails from viewers who claim that amazing occurrences took place while they listened to Lord Maitreyas's announcement which happened moments ago in St. Peter's Square in Rome. Let's go live to Brock Summers who watched the announcement with a group of people gathered at Ben's Café in Santa Monica, California."

"Yes, Suze, it's true. People are claiming that miracles happened while they were watching the amazing events unfold in Rome." Brock stood grasping a black microphone, his white dress shirt neatly pressed. He was ruggedly handsome. The hot California sun had turned his skin a deep tan. He grinned big, his wide jaw jutting from his clean-shaven face.

"This gentleman just told me he was born deaf and has been deaf his entire life. And, as he was watching closed-captioned television in his upstairs apartment, his show was suddenly interrupted. He said that while he was watching the Lord Maitreyas he began to hear!"

"Is that right, sir?" Brock turned to a short, stout man wearing a loud red-and-white-flowered Hawaiian shirt.

"It's true! It's true! I can hear! I can hear!" the little man shouted excitedly. The few white hairs combed over his bald head waved in the breeze. "I was born deaf, and now I can hear! It's a miracle! Lord Maitreyas has healed me!"

A small crowd gathered around the man as tears streamed down his cheeks. A lady put her arms around him, and others clapped. An older black man yelled, "Hallelujah!"

"Quite a story here, Suze," Brock said, looking into the camera. "But there are more amazing stories. I want to take us over to Joe's Bar and Grill which is across the street here in downtown Santa Monica."

He walked out of Ben's Café, and the camera jostled as it followed him into the dimly lit street. Main Street was eerily quiet and empty of traffic. The camera continued to bounce up and down as it followed Brock to a trendy restaurant where maroon umbrellas towered over sidewalk tables. Brock stopped and turned back to the camera.

"Here, a lady claims to have somehow been healed while she was watching the Lord Maitreyas on television."

Brock pointed to a black chair mounted with large wheels padded with rubber. A few feet away a group of people surrounded a grey-haired lady, her face wet with tears. Brock pushed his microphone through the crowd and into the face of the woman.

"Excuse me, ma'am. Is this your wheelchair?"

"Yes, it is, young man!" she cried out into the microphone.

"Can you tell our viewers what happened while you were watching the Lord Maitreyas?"

She smiled, apparently enjoying the attention. "I was watching that mar-ve-lous Lord Maitreyas on television." Her voice was hoarse from years of smoking. "When I heard him tell me, 'Now, Arlene, you don't need that wheelchair anymore. Now, Arlene, get up and walk!' I thought I was going crazy. But the next thing I know I'm getting up out of that darned wheelchair and I'm walking! Look! I'm healed!"

Her body bounced up and down. "I can walk. Thank you, Lord Maitreyas!"

"Amazing stories of miracles here in downtown, Suze." Brook looked into the camera and adjusted his earpiece.

"Thank you, Brock." Suze Graham shuffled papers in front of her. "We are hearing similar stories from all over the city and around the world." Her eyes glistened with tears. "This is truly an amazing day."

....

Less than a month after the Day of Pentecost, the cardinal electors assembled under the hands of man and God, in the high rectangular brick building of the Sistine Chapel. They were charged with the responsibility of choosing a new leader for the Catholic church, the next holy Roman pontiff.

While the cardinals debated behind locked doors out of sight of the media, thousands gathered in St. Peter's Square just as they had during Maitreyas's Day of Pentecost. They anxiously waited and watched the chimney above the red-tiled roof of the chapel. Black smoke indicated the cardinals had not reached a decision; white smoke signaled that a new pope had been selected.

Days passed. Reporters staked out small claims in the square with good views of the chimneys behind them. Several times the crowd let out a loud collective moan of disappointment, and cameras swung to focus on the puffs of black smoke streaming up from the chimney and into the hazy Roman skies.

The world waited for the answer to one, central question: Would the church accept Peter Roma as Jesus of Nazareth? Would the cardinals, draped in the robes of authority and knowledge, validate Maitreyas's claims? Would they put their official stamp of approval on the miracles he had performed and the prophecies he had made? Would they give their permission to the world to follow him and his disciple?

One early morning, after days of anxious waiting, the heavy, ancient bells of St. Peter's Basilica rang, and white smoke curled up out of the chimney. A new pope had been elected.

The proto-deacon of the College of Cardinals stepped onto the main balcony of the Vatican and declared to the world: "*Habemus papam!* We have a pope. . .Petrus Romanus—Peter Roma!"

Becky became disheartened as she watched the cheering crowds. Peter Roma walked onto the balcony; his white linen soutane glistened in the sun, and a two-horned mitra[11] gently covered the top of his wavy jet-black hair. He

---

[11] "And I beheld another beast coming up out of the earth; and he had **two horns like a lamb**, and he spake as a dragon" (Revelation 13:11).

gave an apostolic blessing to the city of Rome and to the world.

The crowd fell silent as his voice echoed off the colonnade. "We all believe in the same Christ. Humanity must prepare and respond correctly to the return of Christ. In order to accomplish this, you must know the truth of God's word. Through centuries God's message to mankind has been lost in flawed translations and rewritings of his holy Bible. Evil men have corrupted its meaning and used it for their own good, and humanity has become ever more distant from the truth and love of God's word."

The crowd stood silent as Peter Roma held a small black book up over his head. "Rejoice, for today I bring you 'The New Gospel.'[12] Destroy your old, flawed and meaningless Bibles. God never intended for it to be taken literally. Today I give you the correct understanding of God's message. It is here, for the entire world to hear and understand. From this book will come the peace and love and sharing which Lord Maitreyas spoke of."

That night Becky sat curled in a ball on the couch, holding a large pillow in her arms. Tears filled her eyes as she watched Brock Summers report on a Bible-burning party from Santa Monica Beach. The sands glowed bright red and orange as people laughed and sang around a ten-foot-high pile of burning Bibles.

A little girl—Becky guessed her to be around six years old—emerged from the crowd holding a black leather-bound Bible much like the one that sat in Becky's nightstand drawer. Its gold letters sparkled against the flames of the bonfire. The camera zoomed in on the little girl as she held the Bible up over her head, her brown hair whipping in the cool ocean breeze. She turned her head and looked up at her father's face. He smiled and nodded

---

[12] "But even if we, or an angel from heaven, preach any other gospel to you than what we have preached to you, let him be accursed" (Galatians 1: 8).

approvingly. With that, she flung her arms down in a wild motion and sent the Bible flying into the roaring fire. The camera followed the book and zoomed in tight as the edges curled and succumbed to the flames. The black leather cover bubbled and warped as the thin pages quickly evaporated into smoke. Becky felt her chest shudder with grief as she watched the gold lettering melt and run down the face of the book like tears.

For false Christs and false prophets will rise and show great signs and wonders to deceive, if possible, even the elect.
Matthew 24:24

Beware of false prophets, who come to you in sheep's clothing, but inwardly they are ravenous wolves.
Matthew 7:15

3

THE HOLLYWOOD QUAKE

Becky's prison was once a grand, old hotel. Years ago wealthy and famous guests paid a great sum of money to stay in the room she cannot escape. The stained and faded Navajo-white block walls are riddled with toggle bolt holes. Eerie patches mark the places where expensive, brilliantly colored artwork had hung, their shadows forever burned into the walls like victims of a nuclear blast. A train of ants snakes its way past an opulent, broken light switch and along the crack of the baseboard searching for meager scraps of food to haul off to their nests. Dirt and bacteria have collected on red frays of carpet that once covered the now-splintered floors. It smells of mildew and stale cigarette smoke.

A grey metal student desk and chair sit below a small window. A brand-new copy of the "New Gospel" sits on the corner of the flat metal surface along with a writing tablet and pen. Becky always leaves the book lying open to appear as if she is studying the text. She hopes it will please those watching her.

Opposite the window a flat pillow and light-blue blanket cover a bulky mattress held up by a squeaky metal frame.

A rotating camera hums and whirs from the ceiling, recording her every move. At times, the feeling of the guard's eyes on her becomes so intense she cannot help but make funny faces at the recording device to break the tension.

The morning sunlight that pours through is broken by a tight succession of black wrought iron security bars bolted to the outside stucco building. It marches across the dirty floor and up the stained walls, marking long, quiet hours. Becky stretches her stiff arms and legs and paces back and forth between her desk and her bed in an effort to get her blood moving. The stale air causes her lungs to clinch, and she gags and coughs. She stands still, laboring to catch her breath.

The distant wail of fire engines comes through the bars of her window. She leans over her desk and peers out. The air outside is hazy with smoke. A helicopter moves quickly across the small patch of orange sky. Somewhere a fire is burning. Her fingers close the window blocking the smell of smoke and the microscopic toxins produced by the fire.

Her body inclines against the wood ledge while her cheeks press against the glass. She stares down into the courtyard at the overgrown magnolia tree decorated with snow-white flowers. She imagines their sweet fragrance. Two grey-brown mourning doves sit on a branch covered with deep green foliage and coo while they clean their black-spotted feathers.

Becky stays there, her face resting against the window, and watches the birds until the sun's deep orange light fades into a dark grey, acrid with thick smoke. Even after the window turns almost completely black and all she can see is her own reflection, she imagines herself lying under the beautiful green tree in a bed of lush grass. The sweet smell of its pretty, white flowers fills her nostrils with every breath of fresh, clean air, and the gentle, melodic song of the birds lulls her into a warm, deep sleep.

The image brings a smile to her face. She closes her eyes and is back in her childhood home in Simi Valley. "One part sugar and one part water," her mother would say as she let her fill the red plastic hummingbird feeder that hung from the tree in their backyard. Together she and Momma would stand quietly, watching through the kitchen window as hordes of green-headed hummingbirds descended on the feeder, their wings nothing but blurs as they darted about and seemed to hang motionless in midair. Within a couple of days they would devour the sweet sticky liquid, and Momma would reach up into the tree to retrieve the empty feeder and hand it to Becky to fill again.

Looking back, the years she spent in that house on Apricot Street were the most innocent and the most secure. She remembers when her family left that house and moved to the modest two-story stucco tract house in Valencia shortly after the Hollywood earthquake when she was only ten years old.

The thought of the earthquake still makes her stomach jump. Everything changed after the quake. Nothing was ever simple and safe again. She can't remember ever seeing hummingbirds after the earthquake.

■■

Becky strained to focus her eyes. The bright white canopy over her bed was shaking violently. She pulled herself out of a deep suspension of consciousness. A cacophony of noises and movements had jolted the peaceful darkness of her bedroom.

She sat up expecting to see David jumping up and down on her bed. But he was not there. She was alone in her room. A deafening roar seemed to come at her from all sides. Her fingers and toes turned to ice while her tummy leaped upward inside her ribcage. She could not hear herself call out for Daddy.

As the fog of sleep melted away, her mind hastily conjured the possibilities. Maybe they were in a nuclear war? The important people on television had talked about it. Tensions between the Asian Union and the North American Union had escalated. The threat of a nuclear strike from the Asian Union was real. *Was this what it was like when a nuclear bomb exploded?*

Everything was shaking and vibrating. It felt like a giant monster had picked up their house and was rattling it like a toy. Her cold hands clung to her pink, ballerina sheets. Suddenly she was tossed to the floor. The thick gold carpet brushed against her face. Her legs were tangled in the pink-and-white striped comforter. She kicked herself free. Her entire room danced around her. The stuffed animals on the shelves danced over the edge and fell to the floor; her bed danced and slammed itself against the wall with repeated thuds; her lamp and nightstand danced; the pictures on her wall danced.

EARTHQUAKE! As if she'd seen the word blazing across a digital billboard, she felt a rush of realization. Her skin tingled as adrenaline pumped through her veins.

"DROP, COVER AND HOLD ON!" She could hear Mrs. Nixon's voice repeating the words over and over in her head. She couldn't count the number of earthquake drills she had participated in at Ronald Reagan Elementary School.

She had never been in an earthquake before, but her mother made sure the family knew exactly where to go in case one occurred. Momma and Dad had decided the interior doors were the safest place to be as they were away from the windows or falling furniture, and Dad assured them he had made the doors sturdy and strong when he refurbished their home.

She pulled herself up and held both arms out as she balanced herself and tried to walk to her door.

She lifted one foot up, and the floor rose to meet it. The sensation reminded her of being on a sailboat, tossed about on rough sea swells rising, cresting and then sliding back down again.

The walls of her room rocked back and forth. Loud sounds of snapping and breaking thundered throughout the single-story house.

Her legs buckled, and she sank to her knees as the floor dropped like a trap door beneath her feet. She pushed herself forward and crawled on her hands and knees.

Her hand thrust out to grab the chrome doorknob. She pulled it open and moved through to the hall. The dark of the early morning draped her.

"Daddy!" she yelled as panic swirled through her trembling body. "Daddy!"

He did not answer.

She stretched out for the doorjamb to steady herself, but before she could grab it the door swung violently and knocked her off balance. She lurched forward and clutched the inside of the door and held on tight.

Ghost-white and teary-eyed, her six-year-old brother, David, emerged from his room next to hers. The rabbit ear of his Willie Rabbit pajamas was stained from the chocolate ice cream that had dribbled down his chest the night before.

"David! Brace yourself against the door!" Becky commanded.

Pop! Pop! Pop! The gunshot sound of windows blowing brittle transparent glass outward was followed by the crackling sound of its falling against the ground.

Becky recognized a prolonged series of thuds as books crashed to the ground from the oak bookcase next to the front door. She felt herself lunge forward as if riding in a car that had quickly braked to avoid a dog in the road. She grabbed the door frame to keep herself from falling out of its protective cover.

She felt David's small hands grab at the hem of her Happy Hearts nightgown as he pulled himself up against her trembling body. She let go of the wood with one hand and pulled David close to her. Together they pressed themselves hard against the doorjamb. Huddling within its narrow zone of safety, they felt the earth undulate beneath them as wave after wave washed through the ground under the house. Rows of family pictures cascaded down the walls of the hallway blanketing the narrow passage with shards of glass.

Then, as suddenly as it had started, it ended. The tumult of noise gave way to an eerie silence. The only sound Becky could hear was the furious swinging of the chandelier in the dining room swaying back and forth, slower and slower, until finally it stopped.

"Wh--what just happened?" David shuddered, his dark eyes wide with fright.

"It was an earthquake--A BIG ONE!" Becky relaxed her tight grip on the inside of the door. "But don't worry. It's all over now." *Thank goodness!* A temporary sigh of relief passed her lips. There was no reason to be afraid now. The earthquake was over.

David moved, as if he was preparing to walk away.

"David, wait!"

Becky turned toward the bedroom at the end of the hallway.

"Daddy?" There was no answer.

"David, wait here!"

Avoiding the broken glass on the ground, Becky carefully tiptoed to her parents' room.

She gently pushed against the solid-wood, six-paneled door, expecting it to glide open, but it was stuck. She pressed harder and jiggled the handle. It shifted slightly but refused to yield. Something blocked it. She shoved until she could reach her hand through the small crack and feel the hard cherry wood dresser lodged between the door and her parents' heavy sleigh bed.

"Daddy? Are you all right?" she called into the darkness.

She heard a deep moan.

"Daddy," she pleaded. "Are you okay?"

"Rebekah," he answered with pain in his voice. "Princess. . .take David and go. . .get help!"

She felt a pounding against her chest. She wanted desperately to see her father, to feel his strong protective arms around her shoulders.

"Okay, Daddy, don't worry. . .I'll go and find some help." She swallowed the lump that had formed in her throat and took a deep breath before turning back to the dark hallway littered with broken pictures. *I must be brave,* she told herself. *Brave for Daddy and brave for David. Daddy is hurt so I must hurry and go find help—*

"OUCH!" David's voice was raspy with tears. His fingertips were red and sticky.

"Becky! I'm bleeding! I'm bleeding!" Tears shone in his eyes as he cried out frantically.

Becky reached out for him as she carefully navigated the dark treacherous hallway. She touched his small shoulders. "David, are you okay?"

He lifted his bare foot. Red oozed from a shred of glass embedded in the bottom of his heel.

Becky studied his injury. "Nothing serious, just a small cut. Hold still."

Becky gently traced her fingers over his heel.

"Ouch!" David flinched.

"David! I said hold still!" Using her fingernails like a pair of tweezers, Becky carefully pinched and removed the fragment from the bottom of his foot. Then with the edge of her nightgown she dabbed the blood clean. "There. That should do for now. We'll clean it and find you a bandage later. Right now we need to go find help for Daddy. *Please,* David, try to be more careful," she scolded. "And don't move until I get your shoes!"

61

Becky moved inside her bedroom door and flipped the pink ballerina wall switch. The light did not illuminate. *Hmm, the electricity must be out.*

The early rising sun reflected a faint cheery glow off the mirror of her white Queen Anne vanity. Her eyes slowly adjusted to the dim light. The pastel-pink upholstered bench lay on its side. The canopy bed was still intact, but the white six-drawer dresser had toppled over. The pink ballet-slipper lamp lay shattered on the shag carpet. Her doll and Precious Pony collections lay scattered across the ground like soldiers cut down in a gruesome battle.

Becky carefully moved across the room, edging around the white hollow closet doors that had slid off their hinges, and stepped inside the small closet. Her clothes still hung neatly, and only a few books and boxes had fallen off the top shelf.

She reached up and pulled a pair of worn blue sneakers out of the pocket of the plastic hanging shoe rack. She set them down and slipped them on over her bare feet. She grabbed her turquoise jacket and pulled it over her nightgown. She returned to the hall then entered David's disheveled room and fetched his Robot Man tennis shoes. She waited patiently while he fastened the sticky white Velcro straps together.

David hurried after his big sister down the hallway. As they emerged into the dining room Becky's mouth suddenly flew open, but nothing came out.

"OH, MY GOSH!" David pulled at her arm almost hysterically. "LOOK WHAT HAPPENED!"

"OH, NO!" Becky gasped. "Momma's special dishes. . .they're all broken. . . ."

Momma's beautiful cherry wood china cabinet lay smashed; the delicate flowered china and the crystal lead glass vases, a wedding gift from Grandma Hansen, cluttered the floor in a heap of sharp, jagged shards.

Becky had helped Dad bolt the hutch down with thick earthquake straps. Now the bolts lay against the baseboard in a pile of dusty, crumbled drywall.

They both stood aghast at the sight of the damage. All the wall hangings and plants had fallen over. The forty-six-inch plasma television had snapped from the overhead ceiling brace and lay face up, cracked on the carpet.

Dad's fifty-five-gallon salt-water fish aquarium lay on its side, with emerald-colored gravel fanned out across the soaked carpet and plastic seaweed tangled with the pirate treasure chest. The deep purple Niger Triggerfish and orange-and-white-striped Clown flopped weakly and gasped in the shallow puddle.

David bent over and picked up the two fish and held them in his bare hands, while Becky rushed to the kitchen to find a glass in which to provide temporary harbor for the dying fish. The white linoleum floor was strewn with broken dishes and scattered kitchen utensils. Every cabinet door and drawer stood open.

She scrambled through the pile of plastic glasses in a heap against the dishwasher and found David's tall Willie Wabbit character glass intact. She leaned over the kitchen sink and tugged at the brass handle. She heard a hiss as air choked and spit out of the faucet. Frustrated she wondered why there was no water. She knew she needed water for the fish.

With the rabbit glass in hand, she hurried through the living room past David squatting on the carpet cupping the fish.

"Hurry, Becky!" David pleaded, his voice choking with panic. "The fish are dying. . . ."

As she approached the sliding glass door, cold, clammy wetness penetrated her sneakers and quickly dampened the soles of her feet. She slid back the door and peered outside. "OH! NO!" she yelled. "The water splashed out of the pool. It's all over the backyard and in the house!" Becky suddenly realized she had become distracted by the

63

fish and had forgotten about her father's urgent cries for help.

"David! Forget the fish!" she said as she shut the door. "Dad is hurt, and we must go get help for him."

"No, Becky. . .the fish will die!" David said fighting back tears.

"Come on, David. We've got to go—NOW!"

"I'm sorry, little fishy. I have to go help Becky." David set the two flopping fish gently in a puddle of water near the toppled fish tank.

They walked toward the front door. The large oak bookcase had tumbled over and lay like a slain giant against the doorway. Heavy books scattered across the dark grey ceramic tile.

Becky grabbed the end of the bookcase. "David, help me scoot this over so we can crawl through."

She squinted her eyes and gritted her teeth as she lifted the heavy case inches off the ground. David let out a deep grunt, and the veins in his neck protruded. The bookcase moved only slightly, creating enough space for them to open the front door and crawl through.

Becky squeezed her small body through the narrow opening then quickly turned and helped David.

Outside, Becky and David stared in disbelief. Their familiar neighborhood was unrecognizable. Thick smoke hung in the cool, morning air. Piles of bricks lay crumbled at the base of fireplaces. Wires hung from the sky and spat bright sparks as they pranced wildly back and forth. Torrents of water gushed through the street and disappeared in a strong whirlpool down the storm drain.

A black funnel of smoke stretched into the sky overhead where the sweet old man and lady lived two houses down. Their house was totally engulfed in bright orange-and-red flames. Becky remembered how the old woman would smile and wave every morning as she walked past her home on her way to the bus stop. She hoped she and her husband had escaped the fire.

"LOOK AT THAT!" David pointed frantically up the street. Hissing blue flames spewed out of the top of a six-foot mound that had pushed up through the asphalt.

"WOW!" he said excitedly. "That looks like a volcano!"

"I think it's a broken gas line." Becky quivered.

She blinked apprehensively as she reached down and tucked David's small hand inside hers. He squeezed her hand so hard that he was cutting off her circulation. She knew he was scared just as she was.

Avoiding the broken glass and sharp fragments that had blown out from the windows, they worked their way down the driveway riddled with large gaping cracks, to the sidewalk.

Becky guided them up the footpath. They passed neighbors sitting in their cars in their driveways.

"Why are those people sitting in their cars?" David asked.

Becky shrugged. "I don't know. Maybe they are just too scared to go back into their homes."

Becky spotted Mr. Johnson standing with some other neighbors at the end of the cul-de-sac.

During summer vacation Becky played with Mr. Johnson's granddaughter, Keiki ("kay-key"), who visited from the Big Island of Hawaii. They played "dress up" in Momma's pretty, long, silky nightgowns, and Becky listened with fascination to Keiki's stories of snorkeling and swimming with the spotted spinner dolphins down in Kealakekua Bay.

Becky felt herself allowing panic to take hold of her as she ran toward the familiar man, pulling David behind her. "Help! Help! My dad is hurt, and I can't get to him."

Mr. Johnson turned and stepped forward, his greying hair carefully combed over the left side of his head.

"Becky?" His brow furrowed with concern. "Your father's hurt? Show me where he is."

65

Mr. Johnson hurried with Becky and David back to the sixties-style, cream-colored stucco house with chocolate-brown trim. Mr. Johnson easily pushed the giant bookcase away from the front door and entered the house. Becky led him down the hallway cluttered with broken glass and fallen pictures to her parents' bedroom.

Mr. Johnson tapped on the door with his knuckles. "Joe, it's Art Johnson. Becky says you need some help."

Mr. Johnson pressed his full weight against the door. It barely moved. He pushed and pushed until he created space just wide enough for a small person to crawl through.

"Becky," he said. "I need you to crawl through the doorway—something is jammed against it. I can't open it all the way."

He carefully hoisted Becky up in his arms and guided her through the small opening.

The room was completely black. Heavy curtains hung over the window and blocked out the early morning light. Becky felt glass and books under her feet as she groped in the blackness. The heavy dresser was wedged between the bed and the door. Her muscles strained with urgency as she grabbed the corner and pulled with all her might. The dresser creaked, and the drawers rattled. She felt the contents shift as the monolith's weight transferred to its side and it came to rest on its shoulders, leaving enough room between it and the door for Mr. Johnson to squeeze into the room

"Daddy. . .I'm here! Daddy! Where are you?"

"I'm over here, Rebekah."

The antique sleigh bed squeaked beneath his weight.

The giant painting of the San Antonio de Padua Mission had fallen from the wall and buried her dad beneath it.

The famous artist had painted with great detail the rugged mountains that backdropped the historic adobe brick church laden with Spanish arches. Ancient oak trees surrounded the church, with webs of Spanish moss dangling from the branches.

"Joe!" Mr. Johnson called. "Are you okay?"

"Yes," Becky's dad answered. "I can't move. I think my face is cut badly."

Mr. Johnson carefully lifted the large expensive painting framed in barn wood and set it on the ground beside the bed.

The room filled with light when Becky pulled back the heavy curtains. She gulped at the sight of blood flowing freely from a large gash over her father's left eye. Dazed, he sat up and looked around him. He seemed to be waking up from a deep sleep.

"Quite an earthquake we had, eh, Joe?"

"Yeah. . . ." Confusion seized him for a moment, and then his mind cleared.

Mr. Johnson grabbed a pillow off the bed and pressed it up against his head. "Here, Joe, this will help stop the bleeding, at least until you get to the hospital. You have quite a gash over your eye."

"Thank you."

Becky felt tears well up in her eyes as she took in the sight of her father. He sat there disoriented in his disheveled bedclothes, blood covering his face, neck, shoulders and chest. The wall above him, where the beautiful and valuable painting once hung, was now shockingly empty. Becky's insides ached. Her world had changed forever. Nothing would ever feel safe and secure again.

Mr. Johnson looked at Becky. His eyes focused on her for a moment; then he turned to her father. "Aw, it ain't so bad, Joe. Looks like you'll only need a couple of stitches! You and Becky and little David will all be just fine. I better go and check on the others in the neighborhood."

Mr. Johnson turned to leave.

"Thank you, Art!" Dad smiled gratefully while sliding his legs over the side of the bed, his white T-shirt stuck to his chest with blood. "Thank you so much! Please tell Susan I said hello!"

"Will do!" Mr. Johnson disappeared down the hall.

His blue shorts clinging to his waist, Becky's dad clutched the goosedown pillow to his throbbing head and stood up. He looked down at Becky. A grin spread across his face, and he patted her gently on her head with his free hand. "Good job, Princess. Good job!"

The grin faded. "We'd better call your mother and see how she fared at the hospital and let her know we're coming over."

After Dad stepped into the master bathroom and replaced the blood-soaked pillow with Momma's good hand towel, he picked up the phone off the nightstand and held it to his ear. He clicked the receiver a few times before tossing it on the bed in frustration.

"Come on, kids!" he yelled. "Go get dressed. We're going to the hospital!"

They all scooted into the dusty grey cab of his dented white truck. "Joseph Silver Construction" was painted in bold crimson letters on the cab door along with his contractor's license number and telephone number. Black rubber bungee cords fastened a silver aluminum ladder to the rusty red lumber rack.

Becky smiled to herself as she thought back to the hot summer days before Dad put the pool in the backyard. He had lined the bed of the truck with clear heavy plastic and used the garden hose to fill it with cold, refreshing water. Clad in their bathing suits and bubbling with excitement about the prospect of having "their own portable swimming pool," she and David eagerly jumped into the icy cold water only to dart back out again. "IT'S FREEZING COLD!" they shrieked and shouted out loud, their teeth chattering and goose pimples popping out all over their bare skin.

● ●

Avoiding the large mounds of earth spewing gas in the middle of the street, Dad pulled his beat-up work truck out of the driveway and headed straight to the hospital.

As the big truck moved slowly west on the Ronald Reagan Freeway, Becky's gaze took in the destruction lining both sides of the empty eight-lane highway. The city she called home now resembled a foreign war zone. She had only seen this kind of disaster on the nightly news. Buildings burned unchecked while bright orange-and-red flames kicked into the air sending thick, black smoke high into the early morning Simi sky. Neighborhood streets had become wild rivers as broken water mains sent rapids washing through homes, strip malls, school yards and out toward the Pacific Ocean. Blue flames shot out of broken gas lines in the middle of streets and parking lots like little volcanoes. They passed an apartment building where the second-story walls had fallen down and buried the cars below it. Sirens screamed in every direction, and everywhere people stood with looks of confusion and anguish on their faces.

They rode in silence and surveyed the damaged landscape. Dad's tools clattered in the metal toolbox when the truck swerved to avoid a large gaping hole in the middle of the street. They exited the freeway and drove down Orange Boulevard to the main entrance of Orange Valley Community Hospital.

"What the—?" Dad's startled voice broke the silence, but he didn't finish his sentence.

Becky turned to see what had caused her father's exclamation and felt her stomach rise to her throat the way it would in a fast elevator.

A portion of the building's second level had fallen onto the first floor. The walls had crumbled to the ground and exposed the sanitized, whitewashed rooms like a child's doll house. In one room a single over-the-bed table

69

stood next to a white-sheeted adjustable bed hanging precariously over a jagged edge, suspended in midair.

Shocked and dismayed, several people stood at the edge and peered over, shaking their heads in disbelief.

Fire trucks and ambulances screamed in every direction, and people ran frantically in and out of the corridors.

Dad pulled into an empty parking space and stepped down on the emergency brake with his foot.

The cab doors slammed as Becky and David jumped out of the truck and followed their dad to the broken hospital building.

He bypassed the elevators and headed straight to the stairs.

They waited as two strong male nurses in light-green scrubs carried a gurney down the stairs with a terrified male patient clinging to the stainless steel side rails.

The metal stairs echoed loudly as they hurriedly climbed to the second level. At the top of the stairs they passed through another door and turned into the nurses' station. Becky fought to catch her breath.

Doctors and nurses clad in solid-white and solid-green scrub uniforms ignored them as they rushed frightened patients up and down the halls in wheelchairs and gurneys.

With one hand still pressing the blood-soaked towel against his head, Dad lifted his other hand and pushed through the large door marked "Pediatrics," Becky and David in tow.

At the sound of swinging doors swooshing open, Momma looked up, her blond tresses twisted in a French braid hanging freely down the middle of her back. She was visibly frightened. The large room Becky had always associated with quiet, medical discipline was in chaos. The sound of a generator hummed in the distance. Alarms buzzed. Orderlies swept broken glass against the linoleum floor. Dusty sunlight poured through broken windows.

Heaps of bandages, bedpans, syringes and blood pressure cuffs lay at the feet of open and tilted cabinets.

Momma's pale and drawn face lit up at the sight of her family, but she did not leave her patient, a young Hispanic boy in traction. Both of his legs were suspended in midair vertically at a ninety-degree angle, his hips and knees slightly flexed.

"Oh, Joseph, kids!" she exclaimed softly. Her eyes filled with tears as she quickly finished tending to her patient's bandages.

Once she was sure the young man was resting comfortably, she ran to her husband and children. Her close-fitting violet scrubs flattered her figure. A gold nametag, "Kirsten Silver—LVN," was attached to her breast pocket.

"Boy! Am I happy to see you guys—and thank God you're all okay!" She stretched her arms wide and embraced all three of them in one big hug.

Momma stepped back, suddenly aware Dad was holding a bloody rag to his forehead.

"Joe! What happened? Are you all right?"

"Yeah. . .I'm fine. . .just a small cut."

"Here, honey, sit down." She directed him to an empty stool.

Dad sat down and peeled the rag off his head. A large two-inch gash stretched wide over his left eye.

Momma stared at the bloody towel embellished with delicate lavender roses. Her brow creased in disapproval. "Joseph, not my good hand towel. . . ."

"I'm sorry, Hon. . .I'll buy you a whole new set!" Smiling, he winked at Becky.

Momma studied his cut closely then said, "Joe, it looks like you're definitely going to need some stitches."

She hurried over to a cabinet drawer and pulled out some supplies.

Dad flinched when Momma squirted sterile water from a bottle into the cut, washing out dirt and soot. She carefully dabbed over his thick brown eyebrows with a cloth soaked in disinfectant. She then numbed the area with a needle soaked with anesthetics. She threaded another tiny sewing needle.

"Momma, wasn't that a big earthquake?" David said as he stared wide-eyed at the intriguing procedure.

She stopped what she was doing and looked at her son. She stared at him for what seemed to Becky like a long while. "Yes, David, it sure was!" She turned back and continued stitching.

Becky noticed a young redheaded girl peeking at them from behind a dark green curtain in the corner of the large room. She smiled and waved at the girl who continued to look at them with curiosity.

Momma continued. "I was all by myself when it hit. I heard a huge roar, and then the entire floor swayed back and forth knocking me off my feet.

"All of the kids—I was caring for about twenty of them—were screaming and crying and carrying on something terrible!

"Then I heard a terrible cracking sound. I thought the floor was going to collapse underneath us—I found out later the north wing had collapsed.

"Anyway, I knew we were having an earthquake so the first thing I did was turn off all the oxygen tanks. Then I tried to calm the kids down." She added, "I didn't think it was ever going to end. . . ."

Momma stopped and picked up the scissors then snipped the end of the thread hanging from Dad's brow and tied a knot. She turned and walked over to a counter and pulled a bandage from the drawer.

IV bottles, bandages and colorful medicine containers lay spilled out of the cabinets.

She crossed back to where Dad was sitting and fastened the bandage to his head.

"I tried to call you on the telephone, but I couldn't get through." She put her hands on her hips and sighed. "Thank goodness, you're all okay!"

As days passed, Becky and her family learned from news reports that the earthquake measured 8.0 on the Richter scale. It was centered in the Hollywood Hills, not far from their home. Both the Hollywood fault and Santa Monica fault slipped simultaneously, causing one of the most devastating disasters ever to hit Southern California; more than twelve thousand people were killed, and more than fifty-six thousand were injured. The economic loss had been estimated at about five hundred billion Ameros.

Freeway interchanges collapsed, and damaged reservoirs threatened to give way, forcing thousands living in their shadows to evacuate. Fires burned out of control for weeks throughout the city. Sixty-five thousand homes and businesses were without electricity for months; 40,000 were without gas, and more than 78,500 had little or no water.

About 58,500 structures were moderately to severely damaged, leaving thousands of people homeless. In addition, damage to several major freeways serving Los Angeles County choked the traffic system in the months following what would become known as the Hollywood Quake. The severely damaged freeway structures forced closure of portions of the eleven major roads to downtown Los Angeles.

Orange Valley Community Hospital suffered an estimated 45 million Ameros' worth of damage. They had safely evacuated 615 patients and 300 staff members. Fourteen lives were lost: four were patients who died when they were cut off from their positive-pressure breathing equipment, and three staff members and six patients were killed by falling debris when the second-story floor collapsed.

Many patients and staff members including Momma were transferred to Valencia Community Hospital about forty-five minutes away.

The aftershocks continued for months. Every tremor wore on frayed nerves and triggered fears of another great quake. Millions left California forever. Many had lost everything, while others were simply too frightened by the ever-moving ground. Many areas would never be rebuilt. Much of the once-great metropolis of greater Los Angeles would stand as an empty and decaying shell for years to come. Dad kept busy for months providing reconstruction estimates.

Becky spent days combing through the mess in her room, salvaging what she could. She was thankful she and her family still had a roof over their heads. Eventually Dad found a nice two-story home in a quiet and comfortable neighborhood in Valencia close to Momma's new hospital. Becky started at a new school and played with neighbor kids in the park behind the house. Slowly life returned to normal. Little did they know that the former government, the "United States of America," had built a prison death camp just over the hills from their new home. . . .

> *And there will be famines, pestilences and earth-*
> *quakes in various places.*
> *Matthew 24:7*

4

THE VISITORS

Since his dramatic debut on the world stage at St. Peter's Basilica, Maitreyas appeared in public more and more. He often appeared with the president of the North American Union. The media followed his every move, and the paparazzi prized his photograph more than that of King William.

He met with the ten leaders of the World Union[13] and spoke before the World Parliamentary Assembly. He pushed hard for his ideas on sharing the planet's resources, and a popular movement called World Share sprang up in all the big cities.

The movement lobbied for a new agency to allocate the earth's resources based on need. Protests and marches

---

[13] Ten Kingdoms of the World Union: 1. North American Union. 2. South American Union. 3. European Union. 4. African Union. 5. Middle Eastern Union. 6. East Asian Union. 7. West Asian Union. 8. South Asian Union. 9. Australian Union.

calling for a redistribution of wealth became common in every capital. World Share launched a major media campaign to pressure world leaders into taking action on their ideas.

Within months a bill authored by Maitreyas was brought to a vote before the World Union. The bill passed by an overwhelming majority while Maitreyas carefully watched from the gallery of the World Union Parliament. This bill created an agency for the World Share movement, even naming it the World Share Agency. Maitreyas was tapped to run the new bureaucracy, and he was given unprecedented powers and resources to confiscate personal assets and redistribute them in an effort to create an equal society.

Maitreyas immediately deployed an army of World Share agents to record and tag personal assets of individual citizens with GPS (global positioning system) microchips. Everything from houses to cars to jewelry and televisions was painstakingly recorded as agents methodically moved from neighborhood to neighborhood, from street to street, from home to home.

It was called the Great Pre-Allocation Survey, and the media hailed the effort as one of the greatest undertakings in the history of mankind. Maitreyas's agency was given unbridled authority to enter private homes and search for any item of value. Many people resisted the intrusion and even tried to block the agents from entering their private property. Few of these resisters were ever shown on the news, and when they were, the swift action of the police was also shown. Doors were kicked down, resisters were handcuffed and arrested, and their property was systematically documented and hauled away in large trucks bearing the World Share Agency's logo.

Maitreyas's plan included calculating the value of each union's total wealth and then redistributing the assets to achieve more equality between the wealthy unions and the less fortunate unions.

If a union's wheat or sugar crop was destroyed by drought or flood, then other unions would be compelled to provide food from their own storehouses to fill the demand. According to Maitreyas, every union would eventually both give to and receive from the World Share Agency.

Many felt the program violated their rights to their property. Stories circulated in the newspapers and on the internet about farmers in the North American Union who had worked hard and produced more from their crops than was needed to feed their own families. The World Share Agency prohibited them from selling their overages for a profit. Instead they were forced to hand their crops over to the World Share Agency to be redistributed to others who did not have as much.

In the North American Union this program met with much resistance from those used to profiting from their personal labor under the old United States government. Many disgruntled farmers quit farming in protest and let their crops spoil which added to the growing food shortage.

Following the tsunami, martial law had been implemented across the entire North American Union.

Decked out in tan uniforms and light-blue helmets, the W.U. peacekeepers patrolled the streets in white SUVs. They mandated a curfew: Everyone had to be off the streets by 11:00 P.M. Possession of private firearms was prohibited. All gun owners were required to turn their firearms over to the W.U. peacekeepers. Anyone violating this order was subject to a mandatory twenty-year jail sentence.

Becky's dad didn't have a gun—just an antique rifle Grandma Silver had given him for his sixteenth birthday.

Nights were unusually quiet. The only vehicles on the streets were the white government SUVs that circled the neighborhood in concentric patterns. Becky would watch them pass by her bedroom window in the late hours of the night. Their red-and-blue flashing lights bounced off the soft pink hue of her walls and cast a spooky glow over Blake Collins's handsome face smiling from the poster over her bed. She knew the big SUVs and the strong men inside—carrying big guns—were meant to provide a sense of security. She knew they drove past her house every night to make sure no one was using the crisis of the tsunami as a reason to hurt her or her family. She knew they were there to keep order and safety in her quiet, unassuming neighborhood.

But every time she saw their heavy trucks slowly pass her window she could not escape the overwhelming feeling that they portended death.

■■■

"Lunch!" A husky accented voice startles Becky. Her eyes blink open, and her mind snaps back to reality.

The uniformed guard slides a large white cup under the door then disappears down the hall.

Rolling off her cot, Becky walks with swift urgency to retrieve her meal. She bends over and picks up the plastic cup with both hands. Small chunks of white meat float in the thin, watery broth.

Still standing at the doorway, she hastily places the brim of the cup against her dry lips and sips the lukewarm liquid. As the rubbery chunks of chicken and water hit her stomach she feels a rush of nausea. She forces a burp. Still hungry, she leans over and pushes the empty cup back through the opening under the door.

Returning to her cot, she tumbles down hard. The sound of the wire springs ricochets against the walls.

Chicken. How she misses eating blackened chicken. She closes her eyes and recalls the last time she ate barbecued chicken; it was the last time she spent the night at

T.J.'s house and was one of the worst weekends of her entire life.

∎∎∎

Becky loved going to T.J.'s house. Her parents were always so nice and always made her feel right at home.

They usually barbecued when Becky spent the night. Mrs. Smith would boil the chicken thighs over the stove then wash and drain the fat down the sink. Then she'd smother them in thick red barbecue sauce. Mr. Smith would turn them over the bright flames on the barbecue until they were burnt crispy and black.

T.J.'s mom would serve up the juicy, savory pieces of chicken with hot ears of sweet buttered corn on the cob and diet soda. Becky laughs when she recalls T.J. always passed on the corn because she hated picking it from her teeth!

Becky remembers when she first met T.J. It was in the main hall at Valley High School. She was struggling to open her locker. She tugged and pulled at the dented metal, but it was hopelessly jammed.

"Hi!" T.J. flashed her shining hazel eyes and dimples. "Need some help?"

Becky turned to find a petite girl looking up at her. Her hair was dyed blond and hung loose on her shoulders.

"Yeah, thanks!" Becky replied. She was stunned by this girl's beauty. "It seems to be stuck."

"Here. . .let me try." T.J. pulled up hard on the locker handle and jerked it open.

"Hey, thanks!" Becky grinned from ear to ear.

"Sure! No problem!" T.J.'s dimples deepened. "Let me know if you need anything!" With that, T.J. disappeared down the crowded hallway.

Becky bumped into T.J. again in history and then in home economics. They soon became best friends.

T.J. was very popular at school and had many friends. But Becky admired how T.J. never let her popularity go to her head. It seemed like everybody fawned over her, especially her senior boyfriend Dennis. Becky thought he was dreamy: tall, with blond hair and brown eyes, and the quarterback of the Rebels' football team—quite a catch for a freshman!

And Becky really liked T.J.'s father, Bob Smith. He was a retired Los Angeles police officer. Mr. Smith was very friendly and never seemed to lack words. He would always stop her and start a conversation about the former government. "I remember when. . . ," he would begin. She always pretended to be interested while she secretly looked about for T.J. to come and rescue her.

Mr. Smith knew a lot about everything that was going on in the government from his pals who were still in the force. When the United States became a part of the North American Union, most of the police officers were sworn in under the new government.

That night she and T.J. practiced cheers, baked chocolate chip cookies and talked about the boys until the wee hours of the morning.

"Hey, Becky," T.J. asked, "how come you don't go out with Johnny Cooper? I know he likes you—he's always asking me about you!"

"'Cause he's not my type." Becky's mouth was full of orange cheese puffs. "He's such a geek! Besides, I like *mature* men."

"Oh! You mean *mature* like my sweetie Dennis?" T.J. laughed and took another bite of her chocolate chip cookie.

"Yeah, right! Like he's available?" she answered back sarcastically. "You know your boyfriend is the cutest guy in school—but I'd never think of going out with my best friend's boyfriend. Besides. . .I like Blake Collins. . . ." Her blue eyes took on a dreamy look.

"Yeah, Blake Collins, the professional football player—he is cute!" A chorus of giggles rang through the yellow-and-white bedroom hung with cheerleading posters.

Becky was glad T.J. had accepted her answer and didn't press her anymore. She knew T.J. meant well. But she found it difficult to explain her feelings. She never felt comfortable with the boys in high school. She couldn't relate to their immaturity. They just didn't compare to handsome, pro-football player Blake Collins. . . .

It seemed as if they had just fallen asleep when Mrs. Smith woke them up for breakfast. "Girls, breakfast is ready!" Mrs. Smith popped her dark head through the door. She was very short and of Greek descent.

T.J. threw on a white eyelet sundress while Becky headed to the bathroom. Becky used the toilet, brushed her teeth then changed into her favorite blue jeans and red tank top. She stuffed her toiletries and pink nightgown into her backpack then rolled up the borrowed navy-blue sleeping bag and tossed it in the corner of the room.

She smelled bacon as she entered the yellow kitchen, grease popping in the skillet.

"'Morning, Becky." Mrs. Smith turned off the fire from under the iron skillet.

"Good morning, Mrs. Smith." Becky smiled.

"Hey, girlfriend, would you like some bacon and eggs mixed with cheese and garlic salt?" T.J. sat down at the glass table, her smile wide and her brown eyes shining.

"No, thanks—I'm still full from the cookies and cheese puffs we ate last night."

"Oink! Oink!" T.J. giggled and snorted while she motioned for Becky to sit in the empty chair next to her.

"Come on, girlfriend. You've got to eat something!"

"Okay. I'll have a slice of that cantaloupe." She reached across the table and grabbed a slice of the orange fruit. She slurped and took tiny bites while T.J. inhaled the scrambled eggs.

After they ate their breakfast, the girls chatted while they waited for Mrs. Smith to fill out her shopping list for the errands she intended doing after she took Becky home.

Bag in hand, Becky hopped into the back of the forest-green minivan and slid next to T.J. while Mrs. Smith climbed in the driver's seat and started the engine.

It was a short drive to her house, just over the hill off Highway 14. The girls giggled and talked as a red sports car flew by them, followed by a dozen screaming blue-and-white police cars.

"Did you see that?" Becky asked excitedly.

"Yeah, it's probably stolen!" T.J. replied.

The rubber tires scraped the curb, leaving a black mark, as Mrs. Smith pulled up in front of the two-story, California-style, stucco tract house. The grass looked healthy and was a deep green from the iron pellets Dad had tossed on the lawn a few days earlier.

After they said their good-byes, Becky jumped out of the van. Standing on the sidewalk, she waved until the minivan disappeared down the street.

With her backpack draped over her shoulders, she turned toward the house. Her lips smiled at the sight of Momma's white car and Dad's beat-up pickup truck parked in front of the two-car garage. She took long strides as she hurried up the smooth driveway toward the front of the house.

By the front door she noticed a potted plant tipped over, its contents spilled over the walkway. Puzzled, Becky squatted and set the pot upright and scooped up the loose dirt.

She wiped the dark soil from her hands on her jeans then ran her fingers under the brown braided doormat. After locating the shiny silver "emergency key" she stood up and slid the key into the lock. Surprisingly the door was not locked.

That's strange. . .Momma always keeps the door locked and dead bolted.

The door squeaked on its hinges when she pushed it open. The bright morning sunshine spilled into the foyer. The Picasso fish and Yellow Tang greeted her, swimming around the live rock begging for brine shrimp as the salt-water aquarium filter gurgled under the low water level.

She closed the door behind her and locked it. Her backpack made a thud as she dropped it on the hard wood floor.

"I'm home!" she yelled, kicking her tennis shoes off with her bare toes. She noticed the rest of the house was very dark. Her fingers flipped on the light switch. Light beamed from the brass chandelier hanging high from the vaulted ceiling. She walked around the house pulling the cords and heaving the white wood blinds up to let in the sunlight.

Her eyes focused on the black numbers on the Simi orange-crate label clock hanging over the kitchen sink; her mother loved old art and antique crate labels, and with some help from Dad she'd made this clock herself. The antique label was a lithograph of Simi Valley filled with orange groves before the area grew into a big city.

The clock read 11:15. Her parents would be awake and busy with chores at this hour, but the house was quiet and still. She was beginning to feel that something was wrong.

Maybe they took Buddy for a walk?

She walked through the kitchen and pulled back the vertical blinds on the sliding glass door. There stood Buddy, her mother's blond cocker spaniel, batting his long eyelashes, peeking through the clear glass. His floppy ears dragged on the ground as he licked his chops, a signal he wanted to eat.

"Hi, Buddy!" She tapped the glass with her fingers. "Where is everybody?"

His big brown eyes lit up, and his short stubby tail wagged endlessly.

Becky's stomach stirred as she thought of a number of scenarios to explain why her family was gone. The door was unlocked, the rest of the house was dark and quiet, and yet their cars were still parked in the driveway. *Maybe somebody was hurt, and they were hauled away in an ambulance?* She paced back and forth as she worked to convince herself she was worrying about nothing, that they probably just went for a walk and forgot to lock the front door. *But how come they didn't take Buddy?* she wondered. *They always took him. . . .*

"Momma? Daddy?" she shouted.

Nobody answered.

The sick feeling in her stomach wouldn't go away. Unconsciously her mind flashed to her parents then to her brother, David.

She prayed under her breath as she headed up the stairs. "Please, God. . .please let my parents and David be okay." She passed the gallery of family photos that lined the stairwell as she climbed to the second floor.

David's bedroom door was ajar, and his light was on.

"David, are you there?" she called as she hurried toward his bedroom.

As she looked through David's door, a shiver of terror ran down her back. "OH, MY GOSH!" She let out a frightened gasp. Her eyes grew wide as she tried to comprehend what she was seeing. All of David's books, toy cars and stuffed animals were piled at the base of the bookcase. His red-and-white Timmy Time Traveler lamp was knocked over, and the white porcelain base was broken. All the drawers from his oak dresser were pulled out and the contents dumped all over the floor.

Dread escalated inside her as she fought the urge to panic. She slowly took one step backward and turned toward her parents' room. She tried to block out the terrifying thoughts of what she might find there.

Their door was shut. "Mom? Dad?" She barely whispered their names then gently rapped on the hollow door with her knuckles.

"Rebekah?" her mother uttered.

"Oh, thank goodness!" Relieved to hear her mother's voice, Becky pushed the door open.

The room was dark, but a large lump under the embroidered amethyst-and-tan-flowered designer comforter told Becky that her mother was still in bed.

"Momma, what's happened? Where are Daddy and David?"

Becky walked to the window and pulled open the wood blinds to let the sunlight in.

"Oh, Rebekah. . . ."

Becky turned to see her mother's blond hair all mussed and her deep blue eyes red and swollen as if she'd been crying all night.

The ornate wood headboard banged against the sand-colored wall, and the bed squeaked as Becky crawled up onto the queen-sized mattress and crossed her legs Indian-style.

"Momma, what's happened? Where are Daddy and David?" Her eyebrows furrowed with worry. She unconsciously held her breath as she waited for Momma's reply.

Stuffing two pillows behind her back her mom sat up; her black spaghetti-strapped nightgown hung on her thin shoulders. She opened her mouth to say something, but no words came out. She just shook her head as tears began to flow.

"Momma, what's wrong? Where are Daddy and David?"

Her mother leaned over and wrapped both of her arms around her and sobbed uncontrollably.

Becky fought back her own tears. She had never seen her mother like this. The sound of her crying sent chills through Becky's body. She held her mother tight and tried to soothe her. "There, there, Momma. It's all going to be okay. Just tell me what happened."

Eventually her mother's sobs turned to sniffles. She dabbed the tears from her eyes and wiped her dripping nose with the corner of the lavender sheet.

"Becky," she sniffled, "they came and took them." Sniff, sniff. "They came in the middle of the night and took David and your father away."

Becky felt the blood rush out of her head, and the room spin. She grabbed onto the heavy wooden headboard to steady herself. Her stomach felt as if it had just gone over the five-hundred-foot drop on the roller coaster at Mystic Mountain. She gaped at Momma in disbelief. *She didn't hear her right. . .surely she couldn't have heard her right. They? Who were they?* she wondered. *Who took Daddy and David in the middle of the night?*

She had heard stories, rumors and urban legends—people being taken in the middle of the night, sometimes entire families, disappearing and never being seen or heard of again. Stories of camps, secret prisons where the government sent radicals, terrorists, rebels.

But why would they take her dad? What could they have wanted with David?

She was almost sure she felt the agony mirrored in her mother's eyes. She could feel her chest tighten and her heart pound wildly pushing blood through her veins. It felt as if someone was trying to squeeze the life out of her. She swallowed hard forcing down the solid lump in her throat that was threatening to choke her.

She shook her head and refocused on her mother.

"Who took them, Momma? And where did they take them?" Not giving her mother a chance to answer she continued. "Are you sure they're. . . ." Her voice trailed off. She felt weak. ". . .Gone?" She couldn't control her tears any longer.

Momma took a deep breath. "It was sometime after midnight. There was a knock on the front door. Your father grabbed his baseball bat and went downstairs. I heard men's voices—then I heard your father yelling. There was a lot of noise and commotion. A few minutes later two men dressed in black came into our room. One man asked me my maiden name. 'Hansen,' I said. 'Kirsten Hansen.' He asked if anybody else was in the house. I told him David was sleeping in his room and that you were spending the night at a girlfriend's house."

"Go on, Momma."

"One of them went down the hall toward David's room. I heard him pull David out of his bed. David was screaming. He was so frightened." Becky watched her mother's face contort with anguish as she recalled her son's cries for help. "The man carried David past my bedroom door to the stairs. I ran to try to stop him, to make him let David go. But the other man hit me so hard. He pushed me up against the wall and threatened to shoot me if I didn't stop.

"I followed them to the top of the stairs. That's when I saw your father sitting in a chair with his hands behind his back. Another man was asking him a lot of questions. Another man was going through our things. He came out of your room with a book in his hands.

"He asked us where we got it. I had never seen it before, and I told him I didn't know what it was. He said it was a Bible, an illegal copy of the Bible. That it was forbidden to have a Bible."

Becky's mind swirled with emotions trying to absorb everything her mother was telling her. *Some men came into our house, they took Daddy and David, and they found my Bible. . . .*

Becky felt her mother's cold hands grip her shoulders tightly. Her swollen, red eyes stared intently into Becky's. Her voice trembled with anger.

"Why did you hide a Bible from us? You knew it was against the law. Rebekah, what were you thinking?"

Becky didn't answer as the dam of thoughts broke through the floodgates and emptied into her mind. *Did those men take Daddy and David away because of my Bible? But how did they know I even had a Bible? Wouldn't they want to question me about the Bible? It didn't make sense. And why did they take David? He's just a small boy.*

Her mother's rigid grip on her shoulders gave way to a gentle caress as she broke down into tears again. Becky held her tightly and rocked back and forth, stroking her hair.

Becky felt as if someone had snatched part of her soul away—it felt like what she imagined it would feel like when someone you loved died. But this feeling was different from when Grandma Silver died. This feeling was real. She felt real physical and emotional pain. She felt a hollow void in her chest.

Becky tried to convince herself it was probably a big misunderstanding. Daddy and David would return home soon. It was a case of mistaken identity, and they probably were after someone else.

The house was eerily quiet, and she became aware of the absent noises: the beeps and explosions of her brother's video games, the thudding sounds of her father's hammer as he tinkered on his latest project at his tool bench in the garage.

Her father was always the strong one in the family. He always knew what to do. He'd fixed every problem she'd ever had. Now Becky trembled at the thought of having to figure out what to do next without him. She searched her memory for someone to call, a relative, a neighbor, someone who could help her find out where her father and brother had gone. But she could think of no one.

For hours she lay next to her mother. The sunlight crawled through the window and turned soft pink in the late afternoon. Her mother shook as she sobbed. Then she grew quiet, and finally Becky heard her heavy, regular breathing as she slept.

As the house grew dark, Becky began to feel numb. Everything she loved had disappeared in one night: her father, her brother, her Bible.

The sun would come up in the morning, and she would have to continue her life without any of it. As she began to drift off to sleep she told herself to be thankful—at least she still had Momma.

The following days wreaked havoc on Becky's nerves. She prayed and waited anxiously while her mother called one government agency after the other trying to locate her father and her little brother. Momma spent hours on the telephone, repeating the same information over and over again when she was transferred from one department to the next.

Becky sat quietly and studied her mother's expressions looking for any sign of news. When Momma hung up the telephone, her face was always shrouded with disappointment.

"They said they had no information and to file a Missing Persons report."

Becky rode with her mother to the police station and helped her fill out all the paperwork for the report. The police officer was very courteous and assured them they would call if they received any news about her father and David. After that, whenever the telephone rang Becky held her breath but was soon disappointed when she learned it was only a solicitor or a wrong number. Her hopes faded as weeks turned into months and still no word about Dad and David. . . .

5

BETRAYED

A deep, angry guttural sound rumbles from inside Becky's stomach. It growls in protest as she turns over and tries to take her mind off her hunger. By the position of the sun outside her cell window she knows it will be another hour or more before the guard will bring her evening meal.

The comforting, clock-like regularity of her meals was the one luxury of her incarceration that she truly appreciated.

After those men took Dad and David away, the money became very tight for Becky and her mother. Momma struggled to pay the bills and provide food. She became desperate and resorted to stealing food from the hospital and bringing it home in her purse.

Still, Becky considered herself lucky compared to the millions who had lost their jobs and were forced from their homes when the global financial crisis plunged the economy into another Great Depression.

Becky and her mother sat in silence at their kitchen table eating scraps of stale bread and fruit her mother had brought home from work. The room was lit by a single candle to save on the electric bill. Only months earlier the house had been filled with the smells of roasted chicken, corn on the cob and freshly baked dinner rolls. The elegant chandelier hanging over the table glowed warmly. She and David would laugh until milk ran out of their noses at Dad's funny stories about his childhood. Momma would admonish him to "stop getting the kids so worked up," even though she was laughing too. Then she would scold Becky and her brother to finish their salads which were piled high with fresh tomatoes, mushrooms, olives and cucumber slices. It was hard to accept that so much had changed in so little time.

Becky pushes the memories from her mind as she again rolls over. Her eyes focus on a round yellow water stain on the ceiling. She tries hard to think of anything other than food.

Food—cheerleading—boys. Those had been the only elements of her universe. Life was simple and secure. She can still hear T.J.'s high-pitched shout: "GIVE ME AN R!"

"R!" Becky would reply at the top of her lungs.

"Give me an E!"

"E!"

They bounced up and down throwing their arms wildly in the air until they spelled out their high school team's name: R-E-B-E-L-S.

They spent hours jumping and kicking. It was their way of keeping in shape and hoping the boys would notice.

Now the only boys to impress are the smelly guards. Becky grimaces at the thought of being touched by one of those Neanderthals.

Fighting back tears, she closes her eyes and lets out a helpless sigh. *Who cares what I look like now? It's not like I have a boyfriend or ever will have a boyfriend for that matter. I'll never be a professional cheerleader. I'll never meet Blake Collins—how depressing. I'm still a virgin and will die a virgin. I'll never get married and never have children. . . .*

"Why was I even born?" A groan escapes her lips. *Dad and David are gone, Momma hates me, and now I'm in prison waiting to be executed.*

Becky buries her head in her pillow as a barrier of tears unleashes their fury.

"Why, God? Why?" she wails hopelessly.

Realizing she is feeling sorry for herself, she quietly prays, "Please help me, God. . .I need you. Please help me to be strong."

Her favorite scripture pops into her head, and she says it aloud. "For God so loved the world, that he gave his only begotten Son, that whosoever believeth in him should not perish, but have everlasting life." The sound of her own voice bouncing off the block walls seems foreign to her.

She lifts her legs over the side of her bed and stands up and wipes the moisture away from her eyes. She takes a deep breath and stomps her foot against the warm floor in a gesture of determination and walks to the window.

The sky has turned dark brown as the smoke thickens. She feels so alone. She wishes she had someone to talk to. She misses Daddy, David and the "old" mom.

She leans against the wall and buries her face in her hands as her resolve melts away and another flood of tears washes over her cheeks.

■ ■

After Dad and David were gone, with no hope of finding them, Momma became cold and indifferent toward Becky. She would leave the house for work before Becky had awakened. When she returned in the evenings she went straight to her room without saying a word.

On her days off, Momma sat on the couch in her nightgown and watched the world news. She obsessed over every development, every breaking story.

Maitreyas was made the top advisor to the World Union which had adopted his ideas for strengthening the world economy through a new monetary policy that worked like a barter system.

The ten unions were linked together under one financial system managed by the World Union Bank. Paper currency and coins were made obsolete.

Units of electronic debits and credits were distributed to all people worldwide. This electronic information was stored in a microchip placed on a plastic card or bracelet with a global positioning device.

This card system and the new "cashless society" were hailed as revolutionary and the beginning of a new age. It was the answer to everything from tax evasion, drug use and crime to poverty and illness. People were encouraged to use their cards for more than just financial data but also for their personal history, health and ID.

With the adoption of this system the familiar Amero became useless. Becky could still remember going to the bank with her father to exchange the family's American dollars for the new, brightly colored Ameros.

The global financial crisis had rendered the once-mighty American dollar worthless. An emergency session of Congress was called, and the Security and Prosperity Partnership of North America Act was passed. Overnight the borders between Mexico, Canada and the United States were erased, and the North American Union was born. Everyone hoped the new government and the new currency, the Amero, would help restore stability and prosperity.

Dad stashed a few Abraham Lincoln and George Washington dollar bills away for keepsakes. He said he thought they might be worth something someday. Now the Amero was just as worthless as the old, green American dollars.

Peter Roma's power reached far beyond reshaping the churches into one universal church. His voice was very loud in politics. He claimed the card system did not do enough to solve humanity's problems. He said people could lose or misplace their cards while criminals could rob and steal the card and wipe out a person's bank account. His solution was to have the chip implanted under the skin. With the insertion of the chip they could also track criminals and locate lost children. He pushed hard for lawmakers to create this legislation. Only weeks before this bill was to be brought to a vote before the World Union, Israel shocked the world by obliterating the city of Damascus with a bomb. The oldest city in the world was reduced to a "heap of rubble."[14] This was a major blow to the nation of Islam, and the world waited for certain retaliation.

But Maitreyas threw all of his political power and influence behind a truce between the nation of Islam and Israel. To everyone's amazement, the nation of Islam agreed. Maitreyas drafted a seven-year peace covenant. Under this "peace treaty" Israel would give the Palestinians land it acquired during the 1967 war and the mountainous southern part of Israel, Judea and Samaria, and in return the Palestinians would allow Israel to rebuild their third temple on the Temple Mount in Jerusalem. The future third temple would be rebuilt on the same site as the former second temple, to the north of the Islamic dome, in direct alignment with the Eastern Gate. This would allow them to "share" the Temple Mount. There would be a 150-foot easement between the two buildings.

While the vast majority of the world praised Maitreyas as the "bringer of peace" and welcomed the treaty between the two bitter rivals with celebrations, some

---

[14]   "Behold, Damascus will cease from being a city; and it will be a ruinous heap" (Isaiah 17:1).

95

Jewish men protested the covenant involving their sovereign and holy land of Eretz Israel and denounced Maitreyas as the Antichrist—the son of the devil.

They preached that Peter Roma was the false prophet of Revelation and that Yeshua, Jesus of Nazareth, was the one and only Christ and sits in heaven at the right hand of God.

But the media did not pay much attention to these protests. When they were featured on the evening newscasts they were portrayed as hate-filled racists who would never be happy under any peaceful settlement.

It seemed as though every time she turned on the television Becky found some incredible new story playing out in some part of the world. So many things were happening, and so much of it did not make any sense. At times she was overwhelmed with confusion. She would walk up the stairs to her bedroom and pull open the drawer on her nightstand before she remembered her Bible had been taken away by the same men who took her dad and brother. She sat on her bed and longed to hold the comforting words in her hands again.

Becky watched in awe when the news reported from Jerusalem that two men[15] with stark white hair and flowing beards stood in front of the Western Wall of King Solomon's original temple where thousands of handwritten prayers were scribbled on pieces of paper and tucked inside the cracks of the huge blocks of quarried stone.

Dressed in sackcloth, they held their hands up high toward heaven and prophesied, "Woe to the inhabitants of the earth and of the sea for the devil is come down unto

---

[15] "And I will give *power* to my two witnesses, and they will prophesy one thousand two hundred and sixty days, clothed in sackcloth" (Revelation 11:3).

you having great wrath because he knows that he has but a short time. . . . The Lord God has spoken, 'Repent of your sins and turn away from the blasphemy of the Beast. . . .' Woe to the inhabitants of the earth and of the sea, because you spill the blood of the saints you then shall drink blood."

The news reports treated the two men as curiosities and speculated as to why they were dressed in sackcloth weaved from goat hair. Some thought they were mourning for the Jews and Christians; others thought they were simply crazy.

■ ■

Becky slammed the cupboard door and set a tall, cobalt-blue glass on the granite counter. She swung open the stainless steel door of the refrigerator and stood staring into cool, bright, misty air.

Earlier that morning she had squeezed a bag of fresh navel oranges and added water and sugar into a pitcher of rich, delicious orange juice. She had let it chill in the fridge for a few hours and was now looking forward to a refreshing drink.

The oranges had come from old man Miller's grove off Highway 126. He had a crush on Momma and would bring her a fresh bag every week when he visited the hospital.

Becky was grateful for his kindness. Since the flu pandemic she was careful about making sure she took plenty of vitamin C, and fresh fruit was very expensive these days.

But now as she stood looking into the fridge she found not the pitcher of bright, orange liquid she had squeezed, but instead it was a dark crimson.

"Momma! Where's the orange juice?" Becky yelled, still staring at the strange red liquid.

"I don't know." Momma walked up behind her. "It should be in the container where it always is."

"What's this stuff?" Becky wrinkled her nose as she pulled out the pitcher.

Her mother studied the container in her hand.

Becky's jaw dropped open. "Momma, look!" She pulled out a plastic milk container. "Everything is red, even the milk!"

"Yuck! It must have all gone rotten." Momma frowned. "Throw it all out before it starts to smell!"

Becky gathered all the containers that had liquid in them and watched the red gooey stuff disappear down the drain. She turned the handle of the brushed nickel faucet. "Oh, my gosh!" she screamed. "Momma, look! It's coming out of the faucet!"

Momma looked in disbelief as thick, red liquid poured from the kitchen faucet and disappeared down the drain.

"Momma. . .what's happening? Why is all the water red?"

"I don't know, Rebekah. Maybe something died and got into our water system? I don't know."

"But it's in the refrigerator. . . ."

Then a shrill noise sounded from the living room. They ran to where Momma had left the television tuned to WNN.

The television screen was blank.

Yellow flashing letters scrolled across the black screen in Spanish and English. "This is a union emergency. We break the scheduled program to bring you the following announcement. Please stand by. . . ."

Suze Graham's familiar face appeared on the screen. Her eyes were wide and her breath quick.

"We have breaking news now. We are getting reports from Los Angeles that the water has turned into a dark-red thick substance. If you see red liquid coming out of your water faucet, please do not drink or touch it! We are unable to confirm that it is not toxic. It could be a health hazard.

"We have reporters en route to the water department at this time. We will bring you information as we get it.

"We are also being told by the CDC that they have collected samples of the red liquid and are conducting tests on it at this time. We will report to you the results of those tests as soon as they are available.

"The police are advising everyone to stay indoors until the nature of this emergency is determined. For your safety, stay in your home or office. Do not touch or drink any red liquid.

"Wait! This just coming in from our reporter at the CDC." Suze Graham's face froze in shock as she viewed the laptop screen in front of her. She looked questioningly at someone off camera, apparently needing confirmation of what she had just read. She then slowly returned her gaze to the camera.

"The CDC has just confirmed that the red substance is"—she hesitated, struggling to form the word in her mind before pushing it out between her lips—"blood."

"Blood!?" Momma asked, unable to believe what she had just heard.

"Ugh!" Becky's lips curled, and her nose wrinkled in disgust.

Suze Graham shuffled some papers in her hand in an attempt to regain her composure. She looked back up at the camera and continued in a calm voice. "We are now going to Brock Summers live at Malibu Beach."

The picture on the television quickly changed. Brock Summers stood barefoot on the hot coarse sand near the shoreline. The sun had streaked his naturally dark hair. His white khaki shorts and blue-and-white-flowered Hawaiian shirt made him appear like he was on vacation.

Behind him sunbathers gathered in swim shorts and biki-
nis.

"Hi, Brock, what's going on where you are?"

Visibly shaken, Brock spoke into the hand-held microphone masked by the large, white WNN logo. "Suze, as
you can see behind me, the ocean here at Malibu Beach has
also turned to blood. . . . That's right—the Pacific Ocean
has turned to blood!"

The camera panned to Brock's right and focused on
a small crimson wave rolling in, sending splashes of red as
it broke on the sand.

Brock was silent for a moment, searching for a vo-
cabulary to fit this strange situation. He then turned to a
young sun-bleached surfer in a black-and-orange wetsuit
streaked with blood.

"This young man was surfing when this strange
phenomenon happened." He put the microphone under
the young man's mouth.

"Yeah, man. . .way cool!" said the young surfer, his
surfboard tucked under his arm. "I was way out there wad-
ing in the water trying to catch a wave when all of a sudden
I saw all of this blood around me. I thought maybe a fish
had croaked or something, dude, so I swam in as fast as I
could—I didn't want to be shark bait!"

"Look!" Brock interrupted the surfer, his finger
pointed toward the ocean. "The fish are dying. They're
floating on top of the water gasping. It appears that they
are dying. . .hundreds of them. It seems they can't breathe
in the blood."

"That is a tragedy, Brock," Suze said, shaking her
head. "We can only imagine what kind of ecological disaster this will turn out to be.

"If you have just joined us we have confirmation
from the CDC that the red liquid is blood. It appears that
all of the water has turned to blood. Do not touch this. The
police have advised everyone to stay indoors.

"We now join our sister station in Atlanta."

"Hi, Suze!" a muscular black reporter stared into the camera cowering under a blue umbrella. "I'm here in Atlanta, and as you can see on the streets behind me. . .it's raining blood! Everywhere is blood—on the streets, sidewalks and cars, and even the pedestrians are covered with blood. It looks like a scene from some horrific horror movie!"

Stunned, Becky and Momma watched, adhered to the television for hours as reports of water turned to blood came in from around the world. The ice caps on Mount Everest glowed red in the early morning sun. People huddled under umbrellas and in doorways as blood rained from the skies in London. No one could explain how any of it happened.

Finally, Momma picked up the remote and turned off the television. The house was suddenly quiet.

"We are all going to die!" Momma cried out. "This is the work of those two evil prophets in Jerusalem. They did this. I just know it. They *must* be killed!"

She slumped over on her side and buried her face in a pillow. The house was still and quiet again. Becky stared at the tiny, black-and-grey image of herself and her mother reflected in the dead screen of the television.

■■

The world fell into extreme fright. Riots broke out in big cities. An ambulance and fire truck rolled up with their sirens blaring to a well-kept house at the end of Becky's street. They were there for most of the morning. She later learned from a neighbor that the family had entered into a suicide pact. Fear and thirst were taking their toll.

Finally, on the third day, as mysteriously as it had come, the blood simply stopped flowing. Fresh, clear water poured from the faucets.

Becky drank until her stomach hurt and stood under the shower and let the clean, hot water wash over her.

The blood had stained the sinks, the toilets and tubs. Even the lawns were stained with blood from when the automatic sprinklers had clicked on. Nothing would get the dark stains out, and soon a horrible smell filled the house. Becky thought it smelled like a rotten, dead animal. Momma brought some green surgical masks home from the hospital for them to wear over their noses to help block out the awful smell.

Then came the flies. The infestation was so bad the government imposed a curfew. Schools and businesses were ordered closed, and insecticide was dropped on the cities from planes.

Peter Roma blamed the two prophets for the unexplained disasters. He called them "the antichrists" and said their destructive negative energy had caused the skies to shut up, creating the drought. He said they then turned the water to blood and brought the infestation of flies.

Peter Roma demanded their deaths and put a bounty on their heads. But several attempts to assassinate the prophets failed and ended in the mysterious deaths of the assassins.[16]

The legend of the prophets grew. They became the most hated public enemies. But, as much as people hated them, they also feared them.

Becky knew the prophets were sent from God, and it comforted her to know she was not alone in her beliefs. She wished she still had her Bible—there was so much more to know.

---

[16] "And if anyone wants to harm them, fire proceeds from their mouth and devours their enemies. And if anyone wants to harm them, he must be killed in this manner. These have power to shut heaven, that it rain not in the days of their prophecy: and have power over waters to turn them to blood, and to smite the earth with all plagues, as often as they will" (Revelation 11:5-6).

She tried to share her thoughts about the prophets and all that was happening in the world with her mother. But Momma refused to take her seriously. She treated Becky's ideas like fairytales and scolded her for not "acting her age."

"Momma, can't you at least consider the idea that those two men on television in Jerusalem are the two witnesses mentioned in the Bible? Some say they are the ancient prophets, Enoch and Elijah! And isn't it possible that all those Jewish men preaching in the streets are the 144,000 from the twelve tribes of Israel?"

Her mother rolled her eyes. "Rebekah, you know what Peter Roma has said. Those two men are wicked and are *not* from God, but of the devil. They're using the destructive antichrist energy to do their evil work."

Becky realized her mother did not understand the prophecies were being fulfilled and knew she must continue to pray that her mother's eyes would be opened.

■■

The familiar scream of the emergency broadcast system sounded from the television again. The yellow flashing letters scrolled across the screen: "BREAKING NEWS."

Suze Graham's face was smeared with mascara. "This is a WNN special report."

Becky's eyes left the outdated teen magazine she had been reading and focused on the television screen.

Suze Graham's voice quivered, and her eyes were moist with tears. "We are sad to announce. . .we are sad to announce the death of the Lord Maitreyas. . . ."

"What?" Becky's magazine fell from her hands and splayed across the floor at the foot of the couch. "Did she just say Maitreyas was dead?" She grabbed the remote control from the coffee table and frantically thumbed the volume button.

"Oh, no!" Momma said from the other end of the couch. Her face drooped as her eyes filled with horror. "It can't be." She placed both her hands over her mouth in disbelief and leaned toward the television.

Suze continued, her face tight, trying hard not to show any emotion. "We are sad to announce the death of the Lord Maitreyas. Details are scarce, but WNN has confirmed that Lord Maitreyas was assassinated. The Lord Maitreyas was pronounced dead at 6:00 EST."

The newsroom behind Suze was a flurry of activity. Reporters and producers were running back and forth, throwing papers to each other and yelling across the room to one another. No one seemed to care that Suze was trying to deliver the news to millions of viewers.

"This just in: the Lord Maitreyas was struck in the head with a bullet. We will report the details to you as we receive them. . . ."

Suze continued to speak to the camera, haltingly, fighting to keep control of herself. Her face was pale, and her small frame shook visibly. She looked as if her own father had been killed.

"We are reporting the details to you as we get them from our reporters in the field. Lord Maitreyas was coming out of the World Union Headquarters in Kufa, Iraq, when a man approached, yelled something to him, pulled out a gun and shot him in the head.

"We now have confirmation that the gunman who shot Lord Maitreyas is also deceased.

"We are being told the gunman was shouting obscenities to Lord Maitreyas. He called him 'dirty

Nephilim,'[17] 'Satan's seed,'[18] and the 'son of perdition' just before shooting him."

Becky stood and began pacing the floor in front of the couch. Her head was swimming.

"Rebekah, sit down. I can't concentrate on the news with you pacing like this." Momma motioned for her to sit.

"But I don't understand this, Momma. It must be a mistake or something." Becky sat back down onto the couch, shaking her head. "This wasn't in the prophecies. Maitreyas was supposed to enter the temple in Jerusalem and declare himself God. That's what it says in Revelation. How can he declare himself God if he's dead?"

"I can't believe you!" Her mother shot a hateful scowl at her. "The man is dead, Rebekah! He was quite possibly the greatest man ever—the only hope we had for a better life. And now he's dead—murdered by some scum-sucking, low-life, religious nut. And you are upset because it doesn't fit nicely into your little roadmap you created in your head after reading a bunch of nonsense in your stupid Bible!"

Becky picked up a pillow and hugged it close to her chest. She had never seen her mother so angry. For the first time ever, she wondered if her mother would hit her.

"That stupid Bible got your father and brother dragged away from me in the middle of the night. And you are still here, talking about it?"

Her mother stood and looked at the television. The picture showed mourners leaving flowers on the sidewalk

---

[17] "The Nephilim were on the earth in those days—and also afterward—when the sons of God (angels) went to the daughters of men and had children by them" (Genesis 6:4).
[18] (God to Satan): "And I will put enmity between you and the woman, and between *your seed* and her Seed" (Genesis 3:15). (Many people speculate the Antichrist will come from Satan's own seed.)

near where Maitreyas was killed. Tears streamed down her mother's cheeks as she turned to Becky.

"Get this through that thick skull of yours, Rebekah." Her mother spoke in a low, deliberate tone. Her teeth were clinched in anger. "That Bible of yours is nothing but a bunch of wild fairytales written by men who have been dead for thousands of years. Those stories have been corrupting men ever since, causing wars and enslaving millions of people. That's why it has been banned, to put it all behind us and let humanity move forward." She pointed at the television. "This is reality. Maitreyas was a man of peace. He was ending war, hunger, poverty, hatred. He was doing what the Bible only talked about doing. Now he's dead. Not because of some stupid prophecy but because of some stupid, crazy person like you who is convinced the Bible is real."

∎∎

Becky spent the next few days in her room. She could not stand to watch the round-the-clock coverage of Maitreyas's assassination on the news. The world was in shock over Maitreyas's death. People mourned by wearing black clothing; her mother did also.

Frustrated, Becky sat at her desk and stared at the blank screen of her computer monitor. Since Momma had turned off the internet service to save money, she could no longer search for impending news. She decided to take her mind off things by calling T.J.

"T.J." The hot-pink phone automatically dialed the number at the sound of her command. She frowned as the annoying voice from a recorder echoed, "We're sorry. You have reached a number that has been disconnected and is no longer in service. . . ." She began to worry that something might be wrong at T.J.'s house. *I hope everything is okay. Maybe Momma will drive me over to her house.*

Yeah, right. Like Momma will do anything for me anymore.

Disappointed, she pushed T.J. to the back of her mind and decided to write in her journal; she needed someone to talk to. She retrieved her journal from its secret hiding place and sat back down at her desk.

Pen in hand she began to fill the blank page with blue ink. *"Dear God,"* she wrote, *"it's been a few days since I've written, and so much has happened. Maitreyas is dead. He was shot and killed a few days ago. I thought he was the Antichrist. Isn't he supposed to sit in the new Jewish temple and claim to be God? This is so confusing. I wish I had my Bible. I wish I could talk to you in person. And Momma—I wish I could talk to her. She won't listen to me when I try to tell her about you.*

"I'm so sad. She actually believes Peter Roma's and Maitreyas's lies. I'm so afraid for Momma's soul, Lord Jesus. When it comes time, please put it in her heart not to take the mark of Maitreyas."

She stopped writing and reflected on her mother's words: "Rebekah! Can't you see? Lord Maitreyas has brought much needed change to our crumbling world. I believe him when he says he can help save our planet from the destructive effects of global warming. Rebekah, all we have to do is become one with him. We're to let him into our true inner selves, and then we will all be like gods!"

She glanced over at an old photo of Momma and her that they had taken one summer at Ventura Beach. They were hugging each other as a large wave crashed onto the shore behind them. The wind whipped their hair, and their fair complexions glowed in the warm sunlight. Her mother's face was so tranquil in that photo.

Becky picked up the photo and laid it face down on the desk. She continued writing. *"I cannot and will not give up on Momma. She's all I have left. I know I must keep trying to share the truth. Please, please open her eyes and let her see the truth, that you are God and—"*

"Rebekah! Rebekah!" Momma's shrill, agitated voice startled Becky. She turned and looked toward her bedroom door as she heard her mother running up the stairs two at a time.

Becky quickly stashed her journal under her pillow and tumbled down on top of her bed knocking a magazine to the floor.

The bedroom door swung open wildly. Momma had tears of joy in her eyes.

"Rebekah! He's alive! He has risen!"

"What?" Becky tilted her head to one side and tried to understand what her mother was saying.

Momma sat on the side of her bed and took her hands in hers. "The Lord Maitreyas, he is alive! He *is* 'the Christ,' Rebekah! Now you will believe! He was dead, and now he's alive. . .he has resurrected!"[19]

Becky had missed the feeling of her mother's warm hands on her. She was stunned by the unexpected news and now understood the prophecy[20] and how Maitreyas would enter the temple and claim to be God. She stared into her mother's eyes. They were bright with ecstasy. She thought of the photo on her desk and hoped her mother would not notice it lying face down.

"No, Momma." She shook her head and suddenly felt heaviness on her chest. She did not want to see tears in her mother's eyes again. She continued as though speaking to a child. "Maitreyas is *not* the Christ, Momma! Jesus of Nazareth is the one and only Christ. *Maitreyas* is the Anti-christ."

---

[19] "And I saw one of his heads as it were wounded to death; and his deadly wound was healed: and all the world wondered after the beast" (Revelation 13:3).

[20] "The son of perdition, who opposes and exalts himself above all that is called God or that is worshiped, so that he sits as God in the temple of God, showing himself that he is God" (2 Thessalonians 2:4).

The sparkle disappeared from Momma's eyes as they narrowed and her mouth tightened. Slowly she gritted her teeth. She leaned toward Becky, lifted her right hand and swung hard, catching her full force in the temple.

Becky felt a hot, sharp, burning pain on the left side of her cheek.

"How dare you! You ungrateful child!" Momma scolded her harshly. "Lord Maitreyas has proved himself, and you *still* refuse to believe?" Her mother stormed out of Becky's room shaking her head. She slammed the door behind her.

···

Her mother kept the television constantly tuned to the news. Becky could not stand to see the stories of the millions of people around the world rejoicing for Maitreyas's resurrection. She fought hard to keep her comments to herself and secretly prayed Momma's eyes would be opened and she would learn the truth[21] that Maitreyas was the false Christ.

Becky was deeply saddened when the news reported that the two great prophets that were preaching in Jerusalem had been mysteriously killed.[22]

Several days after the death of the two prophets Becky and her mother watched in horror as Suze Graham reported on a devastating earthquake in Jerusalem. As Becky watched frantic people running through the rubble-strewn streets her mind flashed back to the Hollywood Quake, and she grieved for the people of the holy city.

---

[21]   "Because they received not the love of the truth, that they might be saved. And for this cause God shall send them strong delusion, that they should believe a lie" (2 Thessalonians 2:10-11).

[22]   "When they finish their testimony, the beast that ascends out of the bottomless pit will make war against them, overcome them and kill them. And their dead bodies *will lie* in the street. . .and nations will see their dead bodies three-and-a-half days" (Revelation 11:7-9).

"If you have just joined us, a major earthquake has struck the holy city of Jerusalem leaving many people dead, injured or trapped under mounds of rubble. About a tenth of the city was completely leveled late this morning when most students were in school. Children are believed to be trapped under collapsed school buildings while others were trapped at work or in their homes."

Momma smirked. "It was probably those two prophets doing their evil work from hell!"

Becky took a deep breath.

"Momma," she said calmly, "what if those two men weren't evil? What if they were *holy* men—witnesses of God?"

Her mother turned and stared coldly at her. Becky continued, undaunted.

"The Bible said God would send His two witnesses to Jerusalem to prophesy for many days clothed in sackcloth; then they would be killed, and they would lie in the streets for several days. And then. . .there would be a giant earthquake. It has all happened, just the way the Bible said it would."

Becky sat perched at the edge of the couch watching her mother's expression intently for any sign that she was listening.

Momma's neatly plucked eyebrows raised, and her forehead wrinkled. For a moment Becky was hopeful; her mother appeared to be thinking about her words. She was not going to dismiss Becky's words as mere fairytales.

"Rebekah, Peter Roma has made it *very clear* that the Bible has been *misinterpreted* for centuries."

Her heart sank as her mother continued, her voice becoming louder and angrier. "What part of 'the Bible was misinterpreted' don't you understand? You really need to just get over it, Rebekah, and accept the new way of thinking. Peter Roma says it's because of people like you and those wicked fundamentalists that this world is falling apart.

"You're *really* lucky I don't turn you in to one of those camps to get re-educated."

Becky could not control her own rising anger. Now her own mother was accusing her of causing all the problems in the world and threatening to send her to some camp.

"Momma, Peter Roma is not Jesus! You are a smart woman. How can you believe he is Jesus? He is the false prophet of Revelation! Jesus *showed*[23] his scars to his disciples to *prove* he was the one crucified! Peter Roma has no scars."

"There you go again." Her mother stood and wagged her finger at Becky. "You are basing everything on that Bible. Peter Roma has *clearly* explained the reason he has no scars—because when he ascended from the sixth ray *he was given a new body.*"

Her mother sat down again and stared at the images of smoke rising above Jerusalem. Her voice was calmer now. "If your father was here, he'd straighten out that thick head of yours. Why are you so blind that you cannot see that Peter Roma is Jesus and that the Lord Maitreyas is the Christ?"

Becky fought back tears, not wanting to cry in front of her mother. She stood and rushed to the stairs.

Dad's voice echoed in her head: *You can tell a Dane, but you can't tell them much!*

As she closed her bedroom door she burst into tears. She pulled the teddy bear her father had given her for her

---

[23] "Then He (Jesus) said to Thomas, 'Reach your finger here, and look at My hands; and reach your hand here, and put it into My side. Do not be unbelieving, but believing'" (John 20:27).

tenth birthday out of a pile of stuffed animals and held it close to her chest as she fell onto her bed.

She had never wanted to believe her father when he told her she was just like her mother. But now she knew it was true. They were both stubborn and single-minded. They both knew how to hurt each other.

Tears streamed down her face as her mother's voice played over and over in her head. "Rebekah, if you hadn't been snooping around on that internet and bought that stupid Bible, your father and David might still be here."

Sadly, she knew the real reason they were picked up was because Jewish blood flowed in their veins. *It's obvious,* she thought. *Then why didn't they take Momma? Duh. . .it's because she's not Jewish!* She didn't know why, but it seemed like throughout history the whole world hated the Jews. *It didn't make sense. After all, Jesus was a Jew.*

She feared her life might be in danger because of her bloodline and religious beliefs. *Luckily I have straight blond hair and blue eyes,* she reminded herself. *Nobody would ever guess that I'm Jewish. Nobody knew. . .except Momma—oh. . .and those awful men that picked up Daddy and David. . . .*

6

THE DEATH CAMP

Becky snuggled between her soft, heavy blanket and light-blue cotton sheets. Her breathing was slow and deep, and she could feel the tensions of the day melt away from her neck and back.

Earlier that evening she'd helped Momma prepare dinner. The house was quiet except for the low sounds of Becky draining the water from the spaghetti into the colander and her mother stirring the sauce on the stove. They stood side by side at the counter as Momma mixed the contents together into a large, glass bowl. Momma had aimed the remote control at the television and switched off the constant stream of clattering news before calling Becky to help with dinner. Becky couldn't remember the last time they had been together without the unrelenting discord of WNN supplying the background noise to their hollow conversation. Now the only noise filling the house was the clacking of the pots and pans on the stove.

As her mother sliced an aged tomato into small wedges she took a deep breath and broke the silence between them. "You remember that softball team you played on and I used to coach when you were nine years old?"

Becky looked at her mother who had not taken her eyes away from the fleshy red fruit. Her face was soft; the deep lines of worry in her forehead and around her eyes seemed to have faded.

"Yes, I remember," she responded. "The Roadrunners. Why?"

Still concentrating on the tomato in front of her, the corners of her mouth lifted into a gentle smile. "Oh, I don't know why, but I was just remembering that time when the umpire made that ridiculous call, calling you out when it was obvious to everyone that you were safe, and how I got so mad."

Becky snickered as the scene flashed across her memory. Her mother's long, blond ponytail bobbed wildly under her green baseball cap. She stomped her foot and pointed aggressively at the umpire then to the Tigers' coach before finally throwing her arms in the air, cussing and plodding off the field in a huff.

"Yeah, I remember all the other girls were so confused and didn't know what to do when you walked off the ball field," Becky recalled. "But I just kept telling them, 'That's totally normal for my mom. She coaches like a man!'"

They both laughed. They continued to reminisce about the good times over dinner and stayed sitting at the kitchen table, talking and laughing, long after the dinner plates were empty. Her mother's sudden cheerfulness was puzzling to Becky. But she reveled in the familiar comfort of her mother's laugh and the warmth of the gentle touch of her fingers as she reached across the table to brush a stray hair away from Becky's eyes.

Before climbing the stairs to her bedroom, Becky wrapped her arms around her mother and embraced her tightly. A sense of peace and security washed over her as she felt her mother's arms around her. *Everything is going to be okay now,* she thought.

As she reluctantly pulled away and looked into her mother's eyes, she detected a twinge of sadness.

Becky curled up in the warm blankets on her bed, the strong, smiling eyes of Blake Collins watching over her protectively. She soon fell into a deep and peaceful sleep.

"Rebekah!" The unfamiliar voice was deep and masculine. "Rebekah! Wake up!" The sounds of weighty footsteps and movement in her room startled her out of the foggy region between dream and reality.

"Huh?" She tried to open her eyes, but the blinding light from the overhead fixture burned. She blinked rapidly and rubbed her eyes as she tried to sit up.

Two foreign men dressed in black shirts and trousers stood on either side of her bed. She could smell bad breath. *UGH!* She hid her nose with the end of the sheet.

"Rebekah Silver?" It was the short man with a pudgy face; his black beret hid his bald head. His large, meaty hand grabbed the sheet and yanked it away from her face.

The violent movement jostled Becky awake. *Who are these men, and what do they want?* A feeling of impending danger rose within her. She began to feel afraid, very afraid.

"Momma!" she called out as she tugged at the blankets on her bed and wrapped them up tightly around her body.

A tall slender man aimed an M-4 automatic gun at her; his thick black hair stuck out from under his beret.

"Get up!" the pudgy man commanded.

"Who. . .who are you?" she stammered, her voice trembling.

"Get up and come with us!" the pudgy man repeated.

Releasing the covers, Becky moved slowly, sliding her slender leg out from under the protection of the bed covers. She eyed the doorway and the hall beyond. She hoped to see her mother come through the hall to rescue her. She thought of the story they had relived earlier that evening, her mother so angered by an injustice to her little girl that she nearly came to blows with the opposing team's coach.

Her bare feet hit the wood floor with a light thud as she crawled out of bed tugging her crooked nightgown back into place. She stood motionless facing the men for what seemed like an eternity. Her eyes darted nervously from the large gun aimed squarely at her chest, to the doorway and back again to the gun. With every glance she desperately waited for her mother to come charging into her room, ready to fight and protect her little girl.

Her mind raced. *Who are these men, and what do they want?*

Suddenly it hit her like a huge boulder crushing down on top of her chest. *THEY'RE KIDNAPPING ME— just like Daddy and David!*

"Scream and yell in case of an abduction," she heard her dad's voice saying. "And whatever you do—don't let them take you because the farther away they take you, the lesser your chances are for survival." Becky knew that if they took her out of the house she would never be allowed to come back.

Terror overwhelmed her, and she broke into a hysterical cry. "Momma! Where are you? Momma!" she screamed out loud and made a break for the doorway.

The pudgy man moved quickly, his large hands circling her upper limb in a vice grip.

"Why are you doing this to me?" she pleaded.

The pudgy man tightened his grip.

"Let go of me!" she wailed. "You're hurting me!" She kicked and squirmed violently, trying to free her arm, but his grip was too strong.

"Momma! Momma! Momma! PLEASE HELP ME!"

A strong aroma of halitosis lingered on his breath as the pudgy man twisted Becky's arm hard behind her back. Becky braced her legs against the doorjamb as the man began to push her through the door.

"NO, I WON'T GO!" she screamed. "You can't take me! Momma, please stop them!"

Suddenly a flash of light crossed before her eyes, accompanied by searing pain deep inside her head. Her vision blurred, and her legs went limp as she slowly collapsed into the pudgy man. Sprawled against his feet, she smelled his rancid breath as her eyes began to focus. The skinny man held the butt of his gun high over his head.

"You are going to shut up and come with us quietly, or I will crack your puny skull open like a watermelon. Got it?"

The pudgy man grabbed her arm and began dragging her behind him like a bag of bricks. Becky tried hard to stand and walk. But every movement made her feel as if she were swimming in glue, and her head throbbed with pain.

As the pudgy man pulled her out into the hallway, Becky looked with hope toward her mother's room. The light in the hallway was illuminated, and she could see clearly down the long corridor to her mother's door. It was cracked open slightly, and a shock of her mother's golden blond hair glistened in the narrow shaft of light.

"Momma?" Becky's lips moved.

The door creaked slightly as it shut and the latch clicked.

Becky's heart moved deeper into despair as she realized the truth. Her mother was not coming to rescue her.

A landfill of confusion dumped into her mind. *How come Momma didn't help her? Did she turn her in? Did she follow through as she had threatened? Were they taking her to some camp to get re-educated? How could Momma do this to her, her own child?*[24]

Filled with hopelessness, Becky stumbled as the two men forced her down the stairs and out the front door.

"Dear Jesus, please help me," she whispered under her breath.

Outside, a single street lamp cast a weary glow on the dark street below.

She heard a rumble as the pudgy man slid open the back door of a black SUV parked alongside the curb in front of their house.

"Get in!" he ordered.

Becky reached up and grabbed the armrest and pulled herself into the back seat of the large vehicle.

The pudgy man slammed the door behind her and walked to the front of the vehicle. He opened the door and scooted into the driver's seat as the other man jumped into the front passenger seat.

Becky's eyes searched for an escape. A black wire grille separated the front seat from the back seat, and there were no handles on the inside of her door. Disheartened, she realized she was locked in, with no way out.

The pudgy man inserted a white plastic card into the dashboard then hit a switch. A high-voltage electrical spark ignited the air-fuel mix in the engine's cylinders bringing the large engine to a roar.

Becky glanced at her neighbor's dimly lit house as they pulled away from the curb and headed down the street. She wondered if she would ever see them again.

No cars were on the road except for white or black government vehicles.

---

[24] "Now brother will deliver up brother to death, and a father *his* child; and children will rise up against parents and cause them to be put to death" (Matthew 10:21).

They crossed over the railroad tracks then turned onto the main highway and headed toward downtown Valencia. As they passed, she glimpsed her favorite taco fast-food restaurant at the corner, boarded up with red-and-black graffiti spray-painted all over the plywood.

As the SUV crossed over the highway and turned left into a nearly vacant parking lot, Becky noticed black graffiti scribbled on the sign of the entrance that read, "WORLD UNION HEADQUARTERS."

The large car parked in front of the used-brick government building, taking up two parking spaces.

The pudgy man flipped a switch then yanked out the plastic ignition card. Stone-faced, he jumped out and headed toward the buildings and disappeared through the corridor.

Becky's head ached. She had an excruciating pain over her left eye. It felt like someone was stabbing it with a knife.

She was scared and tried to think of why they had brought her to this place and what horrible things they would do with her.

She feared they would take her to the back of a warehouse and secretly keep her as a sex slave. The thought of their filthy hands all over her body repulsed her. *I swear I'll kill them if they lay one hand on me!*

Her weary red eyes focused on a giant World Union flag flapping hard in the wind illuminated by the street lamp. Ten white stars representing the ten unions surrounded the blue world, and the olive branch below represented peace. *Peace? Yeah, right.* She rolled her eyes.

Her gaze wandered to the mall across the street; its huge triple-deck concrete parking structure was usually packed with cars. Memories of her and T.J. flooded her mind. They loved to go shopping and hang out at the mall, and on weekends they'd meet there and go to the movies.

The sky was slowly turning white as the rising sun began to show itself over the horizon. The pudgy man arrived with a stack of papers in his hands. He mumbled something in a foreign language to the slender man as he jumped back into the vehicle and restarted the engine. The tires on the big black SUV squealed as it pulled back out onto Valencia Boulevard.

Becky noticed several cars were now on the roadway, signaling that curfew was now over and cities across Southern California were coming to life as shops opened and people made their way to offices and factories in the bright, early light.

They slowly followed Valencia Boulevard west until they turned southbound on to a road that paralleled the I-5 (Intercontinental) freeway. Barren, sharp, jagged mountainous cliffs rose around them as they drove through the Newhall Pass.

As she rested her head against the window and stared at the blurred landscape passing by she thought of her father and brother. *Had they passed these same hills?* She felt her throat clinch and her eyes become moist with tears, and she quickly pressed the image of her father and David out of her mind.

She recognized that they were near the reservoir by the 5 and 405 freeways. She could see the big water tank perched on top of the hill. She remembered how delighted she was as a little girl when at night the water flowed down the hill displaying a rainbow of beautiful colors. What a sight it was! It was bone dry now, probably because of the drought.

The blinker clicked as they slowed down then turned right off the main road onto a dirt road. Glistening silver steel railroad tracks lay neatly on wood ties running along the right side of the dusty road. Dirt kicked up as they sped through the canyon, slowing down when it turned back into a worn paved road riddled with potholes. Large mature oak trees silhouetted against the morning sky sprawled across the hills.

The vehicle slowed to a crawl.

A grey guard shack with black windows stood behind a tall chain-length fence with a gate. About five hundred feet from the guard shack was a wood tower with windows. The train tracks proceeded through the fence and through another gate by the tower.

As the SUV crept closer to the gate, Becky noticed the top portion of the fence had sharp barbed wire pointing inward.

That fence is backward, she thought. *Security fences are supposed to be pointed outward to keep people out, not inward.*

It suddenly struck her so hard it felt as if she'd been hit by an eighteen-wheeler truck. *Maybe this was one of those prison camps T.J.'s father, Mr. Smith, had told her about?* Becky felt a shock of panic run up her spine as she recalled the stories he had told of the camps. He had talked for hours about how the former government, the United States of America, had built hundreds of these camps all over America.

Becky had never paid much attention to the stories, but now she wracked her brain trying to remember the details. T.J.'s father mentioned something about an REX 34 program and something to do with the illegal aliens crossing the Mexican/American border. He said an Operation Orange Slice and Rose Garden something would allow the federal government to take over, and he said something about population control. He also mentioned that in the case of a martial law terrorists would be rounded up and quarantined in these camps. He said they built most of these camps close to water facilities.

She dreaded what lay ahead. She knew it couldn't be good. She felt hopeless, like a lamb being led to the slaughter.

She cowered low in the back seat. The SUV pulled up and stopped behind the wire gate. She slid down low; her blue eyes peeked over the front seat between the shoulders of the pudgy and slender men.

The door of the drab, grey guard shack swung open. A young man carrying an M16 cautiously and purposely strode toward the gate. An armband bearing "W.U." in blue letters was wrapped tightly around his bicep over his olive-green uniform. He held his hand up in a gesture to stop them. His black leather combat boots scudded on the asphalt as he wheeled open the chain-length gate halfway.

The pudgy man rolled down his window and handed the young guard some papers.

The guard looked in at Becky, his sharp nose set deep between his grey eyes and his black hair sticking out from under the light-blue helmet.

She quickly cast her eyes downward avoiding his gaze.

He muttered something to the pudgy man then turned and disappeared into the guard shack with the paperwork.

Minutes passed. The engine idled quietly over the incomprehensible chatter of the two men in the front seat. The door of the guard shack swung open again, and the young man walked out with his rifle slung over his back. He pressed his weight against the gate and rolled it back wide enough to accommodate the big black SUV. Then with a wave he gestured them through the gate.

The tires rolled over the gravel road for what seemed to be several miles until they reached a small settlement of white and grey government buildings and a long, black landing strip. White military vehicles with a black "W.U." painted over the hoods sat facing a large, square tarmac where four Black Hawk helicopters swayed in the wind. A faded black A400M, a beastly military tactical transport aircraft, sat near a hanger, its eight-bladed propellers rotating with the strong gusts of air.

They traveled along the train tracks then passed through an empty field and over a small hill.

As they crested the hill, Becky was puzzled by the sight of dozens of large white freight containers with strange pipes jutting out of the tops. The boxcars were lined up like houses in a subdivision.

Behind the little neighborhood of boxcars, several large tractors sat as though guarding huge mounds of freshly turned soil.

The car stopped just outside the settlement of box cars.

I wonder why we are stopping here, Becky thought.

The two men opened the car doors and jumped down from their seats, slamming their doors behind them.

The slender man walked around the SUV and opened the rear door. "Get out!" His voice was raised.

Becky hesitated. Her arms and legs became as heavy as lead. She did not want to get out. She was afraid for what they had in store for her. They were probably going to rape her then kill her, she imagined. Then they would somehow dispose of her body in the hills.

She reluctantly slid across the back seat and over to the door. She dropped down, her bare feet hitting the cold hard ground. The chilled morning wind slapped her, sending goose bumps all over her body.

"Come with me," the slender man ordered, trying to make his voice appear deep. His hand flew up to his head as another gust of wind tried to pry the black beret from his fingers.

She followed him to the side of one of the boxcars, her arms crossed over her chest to block the cold while the pudgy man walked close behind.

Metal ground against metal as the slender man reached up and pulled hard on the lever, sliding back the heavy rusty door of the enclosed freight container.

Becky kept her eyes on the men as if they were vicious dogs who could pounce on her at any second. She felt her muscles tighten, and she grabbed the top of her nightgown and pulled it tight around her neck.

"Get in!" said the slender man in a high-pitched voice, pointing his long narrow finger toward the open door.

Becky hesitated then dragged her feet to the entrance of the boxcar. It was dark inside.

She put her hand over her nose to try to block the rancid smell. As she stood there looking inside, her eyes began to focus on the shiny metal shackles attached to the wall and floor of the boxcar. She felt her stomach turn over and fluid rise to the back of her throat as the odor of feces and urine permeated her mouth and nostrils. Her stomach heaved violently, and she crumpled over. Clear mucus ejected from her mouth. Coughing, then spitting, she wiped off her face with the sleeve of her nightgown.

The guards' faces contorted in disgust. "Now get in there!" said the pudgy man pushing her forward. "We don't have all day!"

She couldn't bear the thought of going into that awful smelly container. She didn't want to be there. She wanted to go home to her nice comfortable bed. Fear clung to her bones. She knew deep down in the recesses of her soul that somehow she had to get away, before it was too late. . . .

Through the corner of her eyes she scanned the landscape littered with dirt mounds and massive oak trees. She clutched her thin, pink cotton nightgown.

RUN! a voice screamed inside her head. She stepped away from the boxcar.

Both men looked at her quizzically expecting her to throw up again.

She ducked low as she sprinted past the two men.

"Stupid brat!" yelled one of the men from behind her with anger in his voice.

Becky heard nothing but her own panicked breath as the cold air slapped against her ears. She ran as fast as she could, aimlessly through the field dodging sharp rocks and sagebrush. Her uncombed hair whipped in the wind as the muscles in her legs began to burn. Her body heated up as she willed herself ahead. Brush cut into her legs, and razor sharp rocks punctured the bottom of her bare feet.

Her gaze was drawn to a giant yellow bulldozer, its broad blade resting on the ground. Her tired legs carried her over to the corroded metal mass. Her heart was racing, and it felt like it was going to explode in her chest. She leaned over and braced her palms against the worn tracks and inhaled large gulps of crisp air.

Trying to ignore the searing pain in her feet she spotted a large pile of dirt near the trees, with small rocks protruding out of the top of it.

Becky limped to the mound and clamored up the side. As she crested the top her nose wrinkled and her eyebrows furrowed together. "UGH! What is that awful smell?" She gagged at an odor fouler than what she had smelled in the box car.

Her eyes gazed into a deep, dark pit stretching out beneath her.

Small rocks and dirt clung to her nightgown as she slid down the side of the steep embankment toward the middle of the pit.

The smell was unbearable. She felt the urge, but her body was too weak to throw up again.

The sound of screaming sirens off in the distance pierced the morning air. Becky clutched her knees tight to her chest and hunkered down low, trying to make herself invisible, then waited quietly, motionless, hoping they wouldn't find her hiding there.

Something jabbed Becky's thigh.

"Ouch! Stupid rock!"

She shifted her body upward and slid her hand beneath herself and grabbed the annoying object and carefully studied it.

She shrieked in sheer horror as she flung the thing in her hand to the ground. Her skin crawled like spiders running up and down her arms as she realized the object was a human finger. It took all her courage not to collapse in a paroxysm of fright.

Becky bolted to her feet and stared at the bottom of the pit. She suddenly realized hidden in the shadows were the skeletal remains of an arm protruding out of the ground and all around her were more bodies, half buried in the loose soil.

Her worst nightmare was suddenly realized. *They are killing people and dumping their bodies in these holes—and they are planning to kill me. . . .*

Panic-stricken she made a desperate attempt to crawl back out of the hole. Loose soil and rocks tumbled down the walls of the pit as she made her way out of the ghastly grave of decomposing bodies.

Out of the pit she crouched down low and scanned her surroundings. She picked up her feet and ran hard past the tractor toward the hills. She ignored the pain in her feet and kept running farther and farther from the sirens. A startled covey of California quail flushed out of the brush, their black-feathered plumes bobbing as they flew for cover.

She reached a grove of oak trees, their massive branches stretched high up to heaven.

Small beads of sweat ran down her back under her nightgown as she slowed down to catch her breath. Her eyes suddenly lit up with hope as the chain-link fence swayed in the distance.

She ran up to the wire enclosure and dropped to her hands and knees. She hastily clawed at the dirt. The ground was rock solid.

She stood up and studied the top of the fence. She stuck her fingers into the row of holes in the chain fence and began climbing the cold wire.

As she neared the top, a feeling of hopelessness overcame her when she realized the fence was pointed inward to keep people in, not out. She would certainly get tangled in the razor sharp barbs if she tried to crawl over.

Frustrated, she dropped back down to the ground.

"Hold it right there, young lady!" a deep male voice barked. She slowly turned around.

The young, square-jawed guard stood before her. His coal-black eyes shimmered with rage. He aimed his M16 at her. "Put your hands up!"

His tight crew cut peeked out from under the helmet strapped securely under his chin. His neatly pressed uniform looked as if he had never seen combat, and his stiff, polished black boots looked as if he hadn't walked one mile in them.

Becky looked around. She quickly realized escape was impossible. She knew she had to resort to the fact that she was defeated. She knew she couldn't outrun this young muscular man, and besides he had a gun. Becky slowly lifted her hands. With a wave of the gun barrel the guard motioned her to move in the direction of the boxcars.

Becky's bare feet throbbed as they walked quickly through the trees. Occasionally her captor nudged her in the back with the butt of his gun prodding her to move faster.

Annoyed by the visitors stomping through their territory, brown ground squirrels screamed to each other and scampered up and down the giant trees while angry Blue Jays squawked at the passersby.

As they neared the boxcar, the pudgy man stood tall, his arms crossed firmly over his heavy chest. His nostrils flared, and his eyes glared at Becky. He lifted his chubby finger and pointed to the boxcar. "Get in—now!"

Becky leaned over and hoisted her legs up on the cold floor and crawled into the disgusting container. The smell of feces and urine was less intense now. The heavy metal door scraped as it closed behind her.

Becky looked around her prison. It was dark except for a small area where sunlight spilled through a hole in the ceiling made by a pipe, jutted through.

Her eyes began to adjust to the darkness, and the rows of chains bolted to the floors and walls came into clear view.

Startled, she noticed a figure cowering toward the back of the dark boxcar. She moved closer. It was a man. His khaki shorts revealed a deep tan on his legs, and his dark-blue collared polo shirt was ripped on the shoulder. His hands and feet were shackled together. Slowly he lifted his head revealing unshaved stubble on his chin. His eyes were deeply swollen, and purple bruises covered his face.

Becky covered her nose with her right hand as she carefully stepped across the sticky metal floor toward the man.

"Hi!" she muttered softly.

"Hel-lo." The shadowy figure flinched, forcing a painful smile.

"Hey—are you okay?" She squatted down close to the man hoping to get a better look.

"Yeah. . .I'm okay," he replied, straightening himself up. "I just got knocked around a bit."

Becky searched his face: well-cut features, sun-bleached hair, a fine muscled physique.

He looked familiar. "Oh, my gosh!" She suddenly recognized him. "Aren't you Brock Summers from the channel 13 news?"

"Yeah. . .that's me all right," he answered with a painful groan.

On the news he was a strapping handsome reporter. Now he looked like a dirty old bum. She caught herself blushing as she recalled how handsome he was on TV.

"What's your name, missy?" he asked. "And what is your crime?" He tried to ignore the burning pain throbbing over his left eye.

Becky settled down on the floor next to him and leaned back against the metal wall.

"My name is Becky, and I'm not sure why they picked me up. Could be for a number of things. Why are you here?" she asked in return.

Forgetting his pain, Brock reached his shackled hand up and scratched his head as he thought.

"Well, for one thing, I'm a Christian, and I believe that Maitreyas is the Antichrist—"

"Oh, my gosh!" Becky blurted out, interrupting Brock. "Me too!" She couldn't believe her ears. Finally another Christian!

"Wow! I would never have suspected you were a Christian! I thought all the media was biased and under Maitreyas's control." She looked into his bruised eyes and asked, "When did you become a Christian?"

"Well, I'll try to make a long story short!" He smiled, a twinkle in his eye.

He didn't grimace much anymore; he seemed to be a little more relaxed.

"Let's see." He gazed into the darkness of the box-car. "Sometime after my mother died, me and my little sister, Sarah, went to live with my aunt Millie, my mother's sister, in California. Aunt Millie took Sarah and me to church with her every week. It was there that we learned about the Bible and Jesus.

"After I graduated from high school I went to college and then took a job with a news station. I was so busy with my career and life that I never gave God or church much thought.

"When Maitreyas was revealed on the Day of Pentecost, it was as though Pastor James's sermons had come to life! I remembered as a teen I was totally intrigued by his sermons about the coming Antichrist, 666 and the mark of the beast."

Becky sat silently and listened.

"Me being the investigative reporter that I am," he said, chuckling, "I decided to do some research. I miraculously located my Bible that my aunt Millie had given me for my fourteenth birthday, and I read through it several times. I soon realized that Maitreyas was the first beast described in Revelation 13 and that Peter Roma, the so-called 'Master Jesus,' was the second beast also described in Revelation. I needed confirmation." Brock's mouth turned to a smile. "A good reporter needs factual evidence to back his story!

"According to Revelation 13," Brock said, quoting from memory, "'And he causeth all, both small and great, rich and poor, free and bond, to receive a mark in their right hand, or in their foreheads: And that no man might buy or sell, save he that had the mark, or the name of the beast, or the number of his name. Here is wisdom. Let him that hath understanding count the number of the beast: for it is the number of a man; and his number is 666.'

"I knew the Antichrist's name had to equal 666, so by using the Gematria system, my beliefs were confirmed. M-A-I-T-R-E-Y-A-S equaled 666 in Greek.

"WOW!" Becky's mouth gaped wide. "I *knew* Maitreyas was the Antichrist, and now you have confirmed it!"

"Yes, Maitreyas fit every description for the man of sin, the son of perdition. I couldn't believe it either. I wanted to expose the truth so I started an underground newspaper called *Wake Up, America!*"

He continued. "I've been secretly distributing the newspaper, and apparently the World Union got a hold of it and somehow traced it back to me. They came for me in the middle of the night—you know, a couple of guys all decked out in black—just like the guys who brought you here.

"Anyway, I knew why they were there so I put up a fight. I must have made them pretty mad because they beat me up pretty bad. And, well. . .that's how I ended up here."

Becky studied her new friend thoughtfully. "I'm so sorry they caught you and hurt you. Those thugs also picked up my father and little brother. They came in the middle of the night when I was spending the night at my best friend's house. They trashed our house and took my Bible—"

"You had a Bible?" Brock interrupted.

"Yeah."

"Where on earth did you find a Bible? I thought they were all destroyed."

"I bought it on the internet—before the law went into effect. I really missed my Bible, especially when Maitreyas was killed. I was so confused. I had thought he was supposed to enter into the temple and claim to be God. I had so many questions and needed my Bible for answers, and then—Maitreyas resurrected!"

"Yeah, that was something when he resurrected. Well, I don't think he *really* resurrected."

"You don't? But I saw Maitreyas," Becky replied with passionate seriousness. "I saw him with my very own eyes on TV. That's why Momma and I were always fighting. She was *so* convinced that Maitreyas was the Christ."

"Well, I believe the first guy Maitreyas was really a man. Maybe from Satan's seed? I'm not sure. Revelation 13 says the dragon, Satan, will give the beast his authority and power. After Maitreyas was shot in the head and died, I believe it was the devil himself who assumed the image of the body or even possessed the body and pretended to be Maitreyas—then everybody would really believe *he* was the Christ and worship *him*. Isn't that what Satan always wanted? To be worshipped as God? And all those who oppose him will be put to death.

"I think a lot of people weren't really sure about Maitreyas until he pulled the wool over their eyes by suddenly resurrecting. Then Peter Roma convinced the world that Maitreyas was the Christ they were all preparing for."

Becky spoke up. "And that's why the real Jesus of Nazareth warned his disciples, 'False Christs and false prophets will show great signs and wonders that if it were possible they shall deceive even the very elect.'" She brushed back the lock of hair behind her ear that had fallen over her eyes. "So who do you think Peter Roma is?"

"I think Peter Roma is another fallen angel. Who would know Jesus better than the angels who lived with him in heaven before the fall? And they were there when Jesus walked the earth and was crucified.

"And I believe all of Maitreyas's other disciples whom they call the 'ascended masters' are angels too. They are ascended all right—from the bottomless pit! They are all a part of Satan's plan to deceive the world with their lies and trickery."

Becky's mind bubbled up like a sponge as it soaked up all the information Brock was sharing with her.

"What do you think they are going to do with us?"

"They will probably send us to a prison where we will await our trial. We will be found guilty as charged, and then we will be executed."

"WHAT?" Becky held her breath. "You mean they are going to kill us?"

Anxiety filled her body, starting from her chest then spreading out through her limbs. She searched Brock's dark bloodshot eyes for salvation. "Is there any way out?"

"Your only pardon would be to bow down and worship Maitreyas and to take his mark," Brock declared. "Consider yourself lucky—at least we get a trial. That's more time. The poor fellas before us, they got no trial."

Becky leaned forward with increasing uneasiness.

Brock let out a low groan as he shifted and tried to stretch out his legs. "Thousands of people, Christians, Jews and even Patriots—the government put their names on these lists. After martial law went into effect they were secretly rounded up and put onto trains that headed to camps, just like this one, and were gassed to death."

Becky's voice was weak. "Yeah. . .when I tried to escape earlier I found some dead bodies in the bottom of a pit."

"There are hundreds of these secret camps all over the North American Union. I was doing a story on them and was about to expose the death camps when the World Union suddenly closed them. I think to avoid public outcry they decided to at least put on a show trial. If a person is found guilty they would then be put to death."

Becky stared at the floor as she brought her knees to her chest. She fought back the tears that were building in her eyes.

I can't believe this! Why can't people see the truth? It is so clear. It is all in the Bible. No wonder they banned the Bible. Jesus gave the disciples so many warnings to prepare them not to be deceived. What part of "as lightning flashes from the East to the West, so shall the coming of the Son of Man be" don't they understand?

"Never!" she said aloud. "I will never worship Maitreyas. I'd rather die than worship him!"

"Well, Becky," Brock said glumly, "death may be your only alternative. Maitreyas will use fear and anxiety as a way to deceive many."

Tucking her thin gown around her body, Becky scooted down the metal wall onto the floor, propping her arms under her head. She studied the crooked pipe hanging down from the ceiling.

It all made sense to her now. It was just as Brock and Mr. Smith had said. Innocent people were secretly rounded up and put onto trains that headed to these death camps. Deadly gas must have flowed through the pipes attached to the boxcars. People must have wondered what was going to happen to them as they waited, not knowing the containers were slowly filling up with intoxicating deadly gas fumes to kill them. Their bodies were then carried out to the fields then dumped into the deep pits and buried. All of those dirt mounds must have bodies under them. She shuddered.

A tear escaped the corner of her eye. *I wonder if Daddy and David are buried under one of those piles of dirt?* For a moment a profound pain cut through her chest like a sharp knife. Her eyes filled with tears as she sniffed back the mucus running from her nose. She pushed from her mind her terrible loss.

How horrible our government has become. How could so many people believe and follow Peter Roma and Maitreyas? Maitreyas was teaching, "Peace! Peace!" while at the same time he was behind all of the death and destruction in the world.

"I HATE MAITREYAS! I WISH HE WAS STILL DEAD!" Becky turned over into a fetal position. She buried her head in her arms and sobbed uncontrollably.

Metal clanged as Brock's shackle scraped across the floor. He reached over and kindly brushed back Becky's hair with his fingers. "There, there now, Becky. Let it all out. It's gonna be okay."

Becky's sobbing subsided, and a deep quiet settled over the foul-smelling box container. Minutes bled into hours as the small beam of light pouring through the round pipe slowly inched its way across the filthy floor. They both waited anxiously, dreading and fearing the unknown. Sometimes Brock hummed songs to break the dreary silence.

The cold wind howled outside, and the day's light began to dim. The menacing shadows in the boxcar grew darker and larger.

The silence was suddenly broken by the sound of two car engines pulling up outside.

A worried expression crossed Brock's face. Lifting his eyebrows, his gaze fixed on the metal sliding door.

Several car doors slammed.

Becky quickly sat up, tucking her knees beneath her nightgown. She was sure Brock could hear her heart pounding wildly inside her chest.

There was a loud screech as the container door slid open, spilling fresh air into the stuffy prison. Two men dressed in sable shirts and trousers with matching berets, peered inside.

"Disgusting! It smells like a sewer in here!" yelled one of the men as he held his hand over his nose.

The other man hoisted himself up into the boxcar. He was over six feet in height, broad-shouldered with an almost dirty, sandy complexion. Tight faced, he walked toward Becky and Brock. His black eyes glared below his massive forehead. Becky noticed a red scar on his right hand as he fumbled with a key. He bent over and unlocked Brock's chains.

The other man waited outside, twisting up his blond moustache, trying to look insolent and peremptory, shifting his gaze from the rows of shackles to the smelly rotten debris on the floor.

"Both of you, outside!" the tall man demanded, jumping to his feet and pointing to the open door.

Brock moaned in pain as he stood up, stretching his cramped arms and legs. Becky pulled herself up and stood close to him. Her knees began to shake as they walked slowly to the entrance together. The tall man stood behind them and waited.

Brock jumped out first then turned to help Becky out. The tall man then scooted out after Becky.

Standing outside, the mustached man seized Becky's thin arm and began leading her away.

As they walked away from the boxcar, Becky felt a surge of sadness at the thought of parting from Brock. Although she had just met him that morning, she felt as if she'd known him her whole life. She had shared so much with him. She felt so close to him, and now she was leaving him. A part of her soul was ripping away. Without thinking she pulled her arm from the mustached man's grip and ran to Brock, thrusting both of her arms around his neck in a fierce embrace.

Brock sensed her body quiver. Stunned and grief-stricken by her sudden burst of emotion, he felt a sob lodge in his throat, but no tears followed.

Tears streamed down Becky's damp red cheeks, and the mustached man angrily grabbed Becky's elbow and pulled her away from Brock. She sniffled as she turned and watched the other man grasp Brock and walk him toward the parked white car.

Brock stopped abruptly and turned back toward Becky.

She quickly brushed away her tears with her right arm.

"Hang in there, Becky. . .I'm counting on you!" With that, his head disappeared into the back of the car.

The mustached man roughly led Becky over to the parked black car. He opened the door. She obediently crawled in and sat on the leather seat.

As they drove down the dusty road, away from the ghostly prison death camp, Becky wondered where they were taking her and if she would ever see Brock again. . . .

It was granted to him to make war with the saints and to overcome them. And authority was given him over every tribe, tongue and nation. All who dwell on the earth will worship him, whose names have not been written in the Book of Life of the Lamb slain from the foundation of the world.
Revelation 12:7-8

7

THE TRIAL

Becky takes small strides back and forth across her cell. With the back of her hand she wipes the moisture that trickles along her hairline. The relentless sun pounds angrily against the outer walls heating the little room like an oven. The heat seems to radiate off every surface: the desk, the floor, the walls, the ceiling, her small cot. Smoke from the fires still hangs in the stagnant sky and casts a reddish-brown hue over everything.

She cannot escape the stench of the burnt grass and timber. Her throat is scratchy, and her lungs are restricted making it difficult to breathe. She involuntarily expels air from her chest and coughs uncontrollably. The grimy soot scrapes her throat and lodges deep into her bronchial passages.

She stops for a second and forces her mind to try to break away from the heat and misery she feels. Her eyes close, and she visualizes the swimming pool back at home in Valencia. She can see herself floating on the dark-blue air mattress while kicking her feet, the cold water splashing against her face.

With a deep sigh she opens her eyes. The peeling white paint on the wall stares at her, snapping her back to reality. With a groan she walks over to the desk where her journal sits, concealing her most private thoughts. Carefully she flips the book open. Broad curvy handwriting tells the story of how she came to this prison. Her favorite Scripture verses are scrawled over and over again. They have brought her untold comfort in her most difficult moments, and hopeful prayers to God are written like letters to an old friend. She turns to the back of the worn, tattered book. Only a few blank pages are left. She holds one between her thumb and forefinger and tugs on it tentatively. She slams the journal closed and pushes it away. She turns her attention to the copy of "The New Gospel" sitting undisturbed in the corner.

It seems to glare at her, mocking her. In a quick and violent motion she grabs the black book and flings it across the room. It hits the wall with a thud; its thin, delicate pages flutter like wounded birds and scatter across the floor. Her body stiffens, and she becomes paranoid when she realizes what she has just done. She glances up at the security camera hanging from the ceiling and whispers an urgent prayer that no one has seen her act of "blasphemy."

Quickly she moves to pick up the brittle pages and stuffs them back neatly into the loose binding. A shrill cry echoes from the bed springs as she sits down with the damaged book and spreads it open in her lap. She reads earnestly, hoping that anyone watching through the dark lens above will figure she had only dropped their sacred book by accident.

"*The mystery of the Sacred wedding.*" Her lips move as she mouths the words.

"*Christ—the Sacred Masculine and the Sacred Mother, the Sacred Feminine. . . .*" Her eyes scan the small, black print.

138

"By meditating under the Rainbow Path of the Mandala of the Heavenly Jerusalem, you can reach a higher state of Being than receiving the Crown of Initiations. . . ."

"Oh, brother." She rolls her eyes and continues.

"The universal consciousness of the Christ lives in you and you are to do what you see from him. The Son can do nothing on his own; he does only what he sees his Father doing. What the Father does the Son also does. For the Father loves the Son and shows him all that he himself is doing."

A feeling of sadness overcomes her. *I can't believe they quote Bible verses only when it benefits them to contradict their lies.*

She stands up and with reasonable care tucks the book under her arm and walks into the bathroom. She sets it on the corner of the vanity.

Thank goodness, there are no cameras in here.

She sits down and uses the toilet. A giggle escapes her smiling, dry, cracked lips as she pulls a loose page out of the "The New Gospel." *Now I have an endless supply of toilet paper!* When she is finished, she stands and jiggles the chrome handle. The porcelain bowl gurgles, and the contents disappear down the drain pipe.

Becky turns toward the tub. She lifts another loose page out of the book and begins the task of wiping away the muck from the walls and bottom of the tub. When she's finished she tosses the soggy, soiled paper onto the ground. She reaches over and turns the brass knob to release water out of the valve. Rust-colored liquid spills out of the spout and begins to fill the bath. The sound of cascading water echoes off the bathroom walls and stained ceramic tiles.

Her blond tresses tumble over her shoulders as she yanks the orange drawstring out of her hair and sets it on the counter. Her shirt clings to her sweaty back as she lifts it up over her head and then drops it to the floor. Her foot kicks the bright orange top aside.

She reaches over and shuts off the spigot. Lukewarm water ripples as she dips her foot in, one after the other, and then slowly lowers herself into the bath. She leans back and squeezes her eyes shut, holds her breath and completely submerges herself under the refreshing water. Her body tenses as it adapts to the change in temperature. Unable to hold her breath any longer, she rises but keeps her eyes closed.

Drip. Drip. Drip. She hears tiny drops of water as they work their way down the spout and into the tub.

As the rust-stained water buoys her small frame, Becky cannot help but let her mind wander. Random thoughts and images flash before her as aquatic sounds fill her ears.

Finally her mind settles on the image of her black-and-white cat, Buster, perched at the edge of the tub dabbing his furry black paws at the drips of water falling from the spout. *Oh, how I miss my Buster Kitty.* She wraps her arms around herself in an unconscious effort to comfort her grief.

A stray Siamese cat showed up at their house one evening and stayed just long enough to birth four kittens in Buddy's doghouse.

Sadly, when the kittens were just a few weeks old she disappeared. Dad said he thought a coyote might have gotten to her because he'd seen some in their neighborhood on his way to work. The kittens were not weaned yet so Momma handfed them until they could eat on their own and were old enough to give away. "Oh, *please,* Momma." Becky remembers pleading for one particular blue-eyed charcoal-black kitten with a white stripe down the middle of his face. "I *promise* I'll feed him and change his litter box." Momma finally gave in and agreed to let her keep "Buster."

"Rebekah Silver?" A woman's sharp voice jolts Becky out of her thoughts. Her body shrinks as she realizes they must have seen her rip the pages out of "The New Gospel."

"Uh. . .hold on a second. I'll be right there." Her voice quivers. Water splashes on the floor as she scrambles out of the tub. She quickly scoops up the large orange shirt and wraps it tightly around her wet body. Her feet leave wet prints on the tile as she hurriedly walks to the entry of her cell.

A short, overweight, white woman stands on the other side of the bars. Her bleached blond hair is pulled back tightly into a bun.

"Yes?" Becky asks softly, hiding behind her shirt. Her jaw shudders, and her exposed skin wrinkles with goose bumps, partly due to cool dampness and partly out of fear for what this strange woman wants with her.

"Uh. . .I was hot so I decided to soak in the bathtub." She tries to explain her appearance to the expressionless woman staring back at her.

"Get dressed. I will be back for you in five minutes."

The woman turns and disappears into the dark hallway.

Becky stands motionless for a second then blindly moves back into the bathroom. Wild thoughts run through her head. *What does that woman want with me?* A sudden stab of fear pierces her soul. *Maybe they have come to execute me?* Her head becomes light, and the walls seem to sway all around her. Her knees bend, and she grabs the sink to keep herself from falling over. She feels the chicken broth she had at lunch rising in her stomach.

All the sounds in the room suddenly go silent, as though she is holding her head underwater again. She can hear only her own labored breathing and the sound of her blood rushing through her ears. Her eyes moisten. *It is almost evening. . .maybe they want to execute me before sundown? That means I may be alive for only a few more hours. GOD, WHY IS THIS HAPPENING TO ME?* she pleads.

After several long minutes she forces herself to think rationally and push aside these morbid depressing thoughts out of her mind. She wipes the tears from her eyes.

"My momma must have come to get me," she whispers. Her hands shake as she struggles to push her arms through the armholes of the shirt. All she knows is she's sick and tired of this place. She wants to go home to Momma, Buster and Buddy.

"Momma is here," she whispers again, trying to convince herself.

She straightens the large shirt around her body and looks into the mirror. A frightened child looks back at her. She closes her eyes and prays. *Dear Jesus, please help me be strong. . . .*

She takes a deep breath and opens her eyes. Her body begins to calm. She combs her fingers through her tangled, wet hair and then ties it back with the drawstring she'd left on the sink. Her hands are now steady, and her breathing is smoother. She looks deep into the mirror. Her reflection reveals a gaunt and pale face, but she recognizes her father's strength in her expression.

The sound of metal banging reverberates throughout the room as the blond woman inserts a long metal key and unlocks the cell door. Those dreadful feelings resurge. Becky slowly moves toward the door where the woman stands. Becky notices the name tag on her sand-colored uniform, "SALLY."

Heavy makeup pastes her face massed with wrinkles, and light-blue eye shadow is carelessly applied over her small inset eyes. The smell of stale cigarette hangs around her like cheap perfume. Becky thinks she was probably pretty at one time.

"Come on. Let's move it." The woman's hoarse voice

startles Becky. She takes one last look at the cell that has been her home for so long, and surprisingly she feels a twinge of sadness.

Becky follows Sally down the hall and finds herself jogging to keep up with the woman's fast pace. Her bare feet sting as they slap against the wood floor once covered with lush carpet.

They pass through a metal door marked "Use Stairs in Case of Fire" and descend two flights of metal steps that lead outside into a gravel parking lot.

Becky searches for any sign of Momma. Her heart sinks when she realizes Momma is not there to greet her.

A white van with black-tinted windows sits idling in the late afternoon.

She hears a shrill, scraping sound as Sally slides the back door open.

"Get in!" she commands.

Becky climbs into the hot seat. Sally slides the door behind her and walks to the front of the van. She pulls her considerable heft up into the driver's seat and revs the engine then flips on the air conditioner and clicks the lever into drive.

Sitting quietly on the navy-blue seat, Becky glances through the black-tinted windows as the van pulls out of the former hotel parking lot and speeds through the sleepy streets of a small town.

Black-and-brown smoke slashes the normally hazy sky obscuring the view of the Sierra Mountains. Handmade "OUT OF GAS" signs block the entrances to every service station they pass. Storefronts are boarded up with plywood and spray painted with colorful graffiti while clothes hang on lines strung in front of strip motels.

Becky notices very few cars are on the road. People are either walking or riding bikes.

Sally lights a cigarette, and the van tilts to the left as she takes a right hand turn at high speed. They are now accelerating down the freeway. They pass abandoned tractors sitting in fields covered with dry grass and weeds. Miles and miles of dirt farms are sprawled along the highway. Becky barely recognizes the area but soon realizes they are in the Central Valley of Northern California. The lush, green farmlands are now dried, arid wastelands. Dust and smoke blow across the empty roadway in front of them.

The hypnotic hum of the van lulls Becky into a shallow sleep.

■■■

"Get out and follow me!" Sally's voice wakes Becky from a hazy slumber. Becky realizes the van has stopped.

She crawls slowly out of the back seat and glances around at the reinforced concrete columns and empty parking spaces. Fluorescent lighting flickers from the ceiling and against the cement walls. They are in a parking structure of some kind.

She follows Sally through the parking lot to a door. Sally pushes a round mechanism with her bright-red acrylic fingernail.

Ding. The door slides open, and Becky follows Sally into a large elevator. Sally presses another plastic button, and the door closes. Becky is knocked off balance as the rickety elevator ascends to the fifth level. The floor sways under their feet as the lift comes to a halt.

Ding. The door slowly opens. As they exit they pass a man in a dark-blue suit clutching a black briefcase. He nods at them before stepping into the empty shaft.

Fresh paint lingers in the air as Becky follows Sally down a long, narrow hallway. Fluorescent lights buzz overhead as they pass closed doors on either side. Sally stops abruptly in front of one of the doors and fumbles with a large set of keys. She feeds one into the dark slot and swings the door open. Her plump hand flips a light switch just inside the door. "You wait here until someone retrieves you," she says while gesturing for Becky to enter the room.

Becky hears the door slam shut and the lock latch behind her. The small room is silent. She nervously studies her surroundings. Moldy mops lean against the bare walls. Stacks of toilet paper and bottles of bleach line the shelves on either side of her. A dirty, yellow bucket half full with grey water sits on the floor. A roach scurries under the blackened bristles of a broom. A tattered copy of a pornographic magazine peeks at her from behind a box of paper towels.

She sits down and cowers low in the corner next to some dirty rags and stares up at the single light bulb that is screwed into the ceiling and casts a dim yellow glow. Are these to be her last impressions of life? she wonders. Will this dirty, little janitor's closet in some anonymous bureaucratic office building be her last stop before Maitreyas's followers execute her for being in their way? She closes her eyes and fights back tears. The feeling of emptiness, the cold numbness in her soul, reminds her she truly is alone.

She curls up on the dirty floor. Memories of her family fill her clouded mind. She thinks about Momma, how she hopes and prays she will discover the *truth* about Maitreyas. And Daddy, such a simple man! Always bright-eyed and cheery, telling his cute little jokes. And little David, how she misses his sweet angelic face, always pestering her and asking her what she was doing. How she would do *anything* to have him back. . . . If she could only go back in time she would be a much better sister. How she misses them all. If they only knew she was scared and hungry, hidden away in a dirty old closet. How she *wishes* she could go back in time and warn everybody about Maitreyas. . . .

■■

"Good morning, miss." A male voice awakens Becky. She forces her eyes open and sits up. She does not remember falling asleep.

A young, dark-haired W.U. guard carefully looks over his shoulder. "Shh." He places his finger to his lips, and with his other hand he reaches deep into his khaki pants pocket. He pulls out a Danish roll wrapped in a paper napkin and a small carton of milk.

"Here," he says.

Becky sheepishly reaches out to receive the food.

"Thank you!" She is surprised by his act of kindness, remembering she did not have dinner. She is truly grateful and knows he will get into a lot of trouble if he is caught sneaking her food.

"I'll be back for you in five minutes," the guard whispers before turning and relocking the door behind him.

"Thank you," she whispers again. She hungrily consumes the sweet Danish roll. Licking the crumbs off her fingers, her head swirls as the sugar hits her system and her body releases insulin.

She tears open the small carton of milk and pours the silky white liquid down her throat. Somewhat satisfied, she wipes her wet lips with the back of her hand. She begins to feel better now as the protein balances the insulin levels in her body.

Only moments seem to pass before the door opens again and the same young guard stands before her with long chains and metal shackles in his hands. He kneels down and binds Becky's hands and feet. He then helps her to stand and in a strong, harsh voice says, "Come with me."

The chains around her ankles clang as she follows

the guard down the long hallway to a set of large, double doors.

They pass through the double doors and enter a large room set up with tables and rows of metal chairs.

The room is filled with people, some standing while others are sitting and chatting with one another. As Becky moves into the room people stop their conversations and watch her with curiosity.

The guard motions Becky to sit in the empty chair in the back row next to a full-figured, black woman. As she sits on the cold chair she notices the woman and the four men sitting on the other side of her are also shackled and wearing the same orange prison clothes as she wears. She quickly realizes this place is a courtroom.

"Hi! I'm Lo-raine." The black lady smiles warmly at Becky, her ink black hair cut short to her head.

"Hi." She smiles back. "I'm Becky."

"They jus' took a break," Lorraine whispers. "They in the middle of a case. A guy named Brock is on trial."

"Brock Summers?" Becky's eyebrows lift high. "The WNN news reporter?" Her mind quickly flashes back to when she had met Brock in the train boxcar.

"Yes. That him al-right. They a-rested him for distri-buting hate litter-ture."

Becky's heart stirs. Her eyes search the room for any sign of Brock, but she is quickly disappointed when she doesn't find him.

She notices only a few empty chairs are left as the courtroom continues to fill up with people.

Sitting comfortably on a black leather chair behind an oblong table in the front of the room, Becky observes a gentleman of advanced years. Deep lines furrow his face, and his long black robe drags on the table as he scratches the white patch of hair on his head. He peers through a pair of wire-rimmed glasses perched on top of his puffy red nose, and he fumbles over some papers. *He must be the judge.*

Behind him a large oil painting of a pyramid, framed in Coa wood, hangs on the wall. A blue-and-white World Union flag stands at attention next to the oil painting.

Becky notices a thin, young man in blue jeans moving quickly through the narrow aisles of chairs toward her. His red, freckled face clashes with his pink shirt.

"Hi!" He smiles as he hangs his thumbs under the thick black camera strap that drapes heavily around his neck. "Are you Rebekah Silver?"

"Yes."

"My name is Bob Brown. I'm here with the *North American Times*. May I ask you a few questions?"

"I. . .I guess so."

"Rebekah. . .how does it make you feel knowing you may be executed?"

"What?" The question stuns her.

"NO TALKING TO THE PRISONERS!" a W.U. guard barks angrily from his post at the doorway, "OR I WILL PLACE YOU UNDER ARREST!" The courtroom falls silent, and all eyes turn toward Becky and the reporter.

Red-faced, Bob Brown salutes the guard with his right hand. "I beg your pardon, sir." He backs away to an empty chair in the front row.

Slowly conversations start back up. Becky bites her fingernails and jiggles one knee up and down as tension builds inside her. She wonders where Brock is and what is going to happen next.

"Quiet, please! Please be quiet. Please take your seats," a court officer says loudly.

The judge tips his chair back and crosses his arms as he looks over the courtroom.

The room becomes quiet.

A strawberry-blond court reporter sits at a small table, her fingers resting on the keyboard ready to transcribe the proceedings.

All heads turn toward the entryway. Becky holds her breath. A W.U. guard escorts Brock Summers, in a short-sleeve orange cotton jumpsuit, through the large double doors, his hands and feet bound together.

Despite his gaunt appearance Becky thinks he looks much better than he did the last time she saw him in the boxcar. His eyes are no longer swollen, the bruises on his face have healed, and the stubble on his face has grown into a thick brown beard. He looks quite handsome.

The guard maintains a tight grip on Brock's arm as they walk down the middle aisle.

Becky's stomach flutters as they near her.

As Brock passes, he glances in her direction. Instantly his eyes light up as he recognizes Becky. His lips break into a smile, and he winks.

Becky's eyes twinkle as she grins back at Brock. A feeling of peace sweeps over her.

The W.U. guard directs Brock in front to an empty chair placed next to the oblong table facing the people.

"All rise," commands the court clerk.

Sounds of rustling noises fill the room as everyone stands to their feet.

"For the record," the court clerk continues as the court reporter begins tapping on the keyboard of the steno-type machine, "the honorable Judge William Davis presides over case #BLS239029, the World Union vs. Brock Lee Summers. The defendant Brock Lee Summers is back on the stand. The court is now in session."

"You may sit down," the judge says as he straightens a pile of papers in front of him.

As the people sit back in their seats, they focus their attention to the front of the room where Brock sits in a small grey chair.

A man stands and approaches Brock. He is a tall, thin, distinguished-looking man with a commanding presence. His thick dark hair hangs limply over his ears.

"Brock. . .before we went to break"—he straightens the vest of his perfectly tailored, brown Piero Lombardi suit—"we were about to conclude the evidence that linked you to the hate literature you have been distributing."

He turns to the table and picks up a clear plastic bag containing a small piece of white paper.

"Brock, didn't you testify earlier that you bought a computer and printer with your credit card on June 14?"

The prosecutor holds up the clear bag for all to see. Becky recognizes the small chit as a credit card receipt.

"Yes, sir, I did."

The prosecutor sets the evidence down on the table and picks up another, larger bag.

"For the record, please enter exhibit K." He holds the clear plastic bag up for everyone to see. A white piece of paper headlined *"Wake Up, America!"* is plastered in black ink.

"This piece of paper defaming the government of the World Union has a secret ID code on it. When held up to a special light it reveals the ID that matches the printer it was printed on." He sets the bag down on the table and picks up another.

"Please enter exhibit L.

"As you can see"—he holds up the bag—"this contains an enlarged photocopy of the code imprinted on the original paper. The ID was traced back to the printer you had purchased on June 14. As demonstrated in exhibits C and D your computer was confirmed to also have hate material on it."

Becky leans in closer, trying to follow the man's rambling monologue.

A look of uneasiness crosses Brock's face.

"You know, Brock, owning and/or distributing hate propaganda against the World Union is against the law and is punishable by death, and the evidence brought before this court is piled a mile high against you!"

He stops, and his dark hazel eyes look

sympathetically down at Brock.

"It would be such a waste for a talented young reporter such as you to throw his life away for such hateful and ridiculous lies. I don't want to see you die, the judge does not want to see you die, and Lord Maitreyas does not want to see you die. Brock, do *you* want to die"?

"No." Brock shakes his head. "I. . .I don't want to die."[25]

"Then let Lord Maitreyas—the Christ—spare your life, Brock." The prosecutor bends his knees and squats down next to Brock's chair. He speaks softly into his ear. "All you have to do is *believe* in him and take his mark as a symbol of your loyalty!"

The room is quiet. No one moves except the prosecutor who stands back to his feet. Becky feels her breathing stop as she waits to hear Brock's response.

Perspiration builds on Brock's temple. He blindly stares down at the frayed green carpet searching his mind for an answer. He tries to compose himself as his shackled hand wipes away a tear that has escaped his watery eye. His shoulders shake, and his face contorts with agony.

Becky wrings her hands in her lap. She thinks of the talk they had had in the boxcar, how strong and determined Brock had been despite his wounds and everything he had lost.

A loud voice from the middle of the room breaks the tension. "You fool! Take the mark, or they'll kill you!"

Brock fights back tears and the urge to sob uncontrollably.

A war is brewing over his soul in the depths of his head.

Be strong, Brock. A firm but soothing voice appeals

---

[25] "And do not fear those who kill the body but cannot kill the soul. But rather fear him who is able to destroy both soul and body in hell" (Matthew 10:28).

to his mind. *Jesus is counting on you.*

You fool, Brock! All you have to do is take the mark! If you don't. . .THEY WILL KILL YOU! The devilish taunt rings in his head followed by evil laughter.

Brock perspires from anxiety.

Save yourself, you fool. . .just take the mark! Besides, what has 'your' Jesus done for you anyway?

Brock! Be strong! Jesus loves you so much that he sacrificed himself for you so that after death you will have eternal life with him. Please, Brock! Don't deny Jesus, or he will deny you in front of the heavenly Father. . . .

Where was your Jesus when you were a child, Brock, when your good-for-nothing father drank and drove your deranged mother to suicide? Then you were sent to live with that Bible-thumping lunatic aunt of yours! A sound of demonic snickering echoes in his ears. *Where was he then when you needed him the most, and where is he now?*

Brock could almost hear his father's cruel voice slurring vile obscenities at him and his mother after a long night of drinking. Terrifying images of his helpless mother, black-and-blue marks on her swollen face from his brutal beating, flashes in his mind. He feels searing pain as he relives the moment she placed the barrel of a pistol to her head and blew her brains out while he and his baby sister, Sarah, looked on.

"We're waiting, Mr. Summers." The prosecutor taps his foot impatiently.

The battle in Brock's mind rages on.

Don't take the mark, Brock, or you will spend eternity in hell!

You fool! What are you waiting for? Everybody else is doing it, and they all seem to be fine.

Brock looks up at the faces in the crowd before him. He slowly bends over and lets out a long, agonized wail that fills the room. Becky cringes at the sound and fights the urge to cry with him. She can see he is in such mental distress.

"We all know your pain, Brock," the prosecutor says. "I know the pain and confusion in your heart right now. Everyone in this room has felt the pain you feel."

He walks over and gently places his right hand on the back of Brock's shoulder. "Maitreyas is here, Brock. Maitreyas doesn't ask for your devotion in return for a vague promise of comfort in the next life. We all have found comfort with Maitreyas right here, right now, in this life. And Maitreyas offers that same promise to you, Brock." He strokes the back of Brock's head like a father comforting his wayward boy. He catches the judge's glare and quickly removes his hand from Brock's head.

He continues. "Maitreyas has brought order to our world. He's ending our wars and feeding our hungry. He is real, and he is here. The evil forces in our universe know it, Brock. That's why they are trying to use you to poison all the good he has done. We cannot let them, or you, do that, Brock."

He straightens his jacket and tie then speaks loudly and officiously. "That's why you get only this one chance, Brock." For the first time Becky notices anger in the prosecutor's voice. "Accept Maitreyas as your lord and savior. Take his mark. Or be put to death."

Becky leans forward, straining her ears. The room is quiet, and all eyes are on Brock. The silence stretches into what seems like long minutes.

"Mr. Summers, we're waiting." The judge snorts as if clearing his nose. "For the record, what is your decision?"

Trembling, Brock squeezes his eyes shut. Becky sees him mouth the words, *Please forgive me, God.*

Then, speaking like a scolded child, he whimpers, "I will take the mark."

Becky gasps. "What?" Her body feels as if it has just impacted in a head-on car collision.

"Oh, no!" Lorraine blurts out loud, shaking her head back and forth. "He jus' sole his soul to the devil."

The room erupts into applause. The prosecutor claps his hands together; a proud smile crosses his face as he shoots a conspicuous wink to his dark-haired assistant.

Shocked, Becky stares blankly at Brock.

"Order!" the judge yells, banging his gavel. "Order now!"

The room falls silent.

"Brock. . .does this mean you will renounce your faith and accept Lord Maitreyas as your lord and Christ?" The judge's unruly grey eyebrows are visible over the edge of his glasses.

"I will," he replies somberly, not taking his eyes from the floor.

Another burst of applause fills the room. There is a stabbing pain underneath Becky's ribs. It feels like someone has reached a bare hand into her chest and is pulling out her heart. She closes her eyes and tries to block the sounds of cheering. She can't understand how Brock can do this. He seemed so strong in his faith when they met in the boxcar. She remembers how they talked for hours and how smart he was quoting Bibles verses. How could Brock renounce Jesus just like that?

"Praise Lord Maitreyas!" says one person in a jovial voice.

"Welcome, Brother Brock!" shouts another.

"Order!" The judge bangs the black gavel hard on the table. It is apparent his patience is running thin. The crowd sits quiet and straight like school children reprimanded by a stern headmaster.

The judge hands Brock's file to the bailiff. "Take Mr. Summers outside to the statue so he may bow down and worship the image of Christ Lord Maitreyas. Then release his shackles and set up an appointment with his probation officer for the implantation of his World Union approved microchip. I want to see Mr. Summers back here in my court in ninety days!"

He raps the gavel signaling the finality of Brock's decision.

The court clerk hands the judge another manila folder. As the judge busily thumbs through the paperwork enclosed in the new file, Brock[26] leaves the stand. As he follows the bailiff, he stares at the floor, careful not to look at anyone. Becky keeps her gaze locked on him, hoping he will look at her. Brock purposely evades her, keeping his eyes fixed on the ground. He shuffles down the center aisle, past her, and out the courtroom, not once lifting his eyes.

Becky shakes her head and whispers under her breath, "I was so sure Brock would deny Maitreyas—*not Jesus!*" A single tear runs down her cheek. "I am so sad for him. . . ."

Lorraine turns her head toward Becky. "I'se sorry, honey," she says sympathetically. "Som'times folks seem t' be strong Christians on the outside, knowin' a good bit of the Bible,[27] quotin' scriptures, and so on. But on the inside, where it surely counts a heap more, their faith is very weak. Only *God* knows a person's heart."

"Yeah. . .I guess so. . . ."

With her brows furrowed Lorraine closes her eyes and lifts her palms upright and prays silently as water

[26] "If anyone worships the beast and his image, and receives *his* mark on his forehead or on his hand, he himself shall also drink of the wine of the wrath of God. . .He shall be tormented with fire and brimstone in the presence of the holy angels and in the presence of the Lamb. And the smoke of their torment ascends forever and ever; and they have no rest day or night, who worship the beast and his image, and whoever receives the mark of his name" (Revelation 14:9-11).
[27] "When they hear the word, immediately receive it with gladness; and they have no root in themselves, and so endure only for a time. Afterward, when tribulation or persecution arises for the word's sake, immediately they stumble" (Mark 4:16-17).

streams down her dark cheeks.

Becky realizes she is praying and decides to do the same. She lowers her head, shuts her eyes and whispers, "Dear Jesus, please give us all courage and strength not to fall apart like Brock did. . .and please give me the right words. . .for I do not know what to say or how to defend myself. Please be with me. In your precious name, amen."

Instantly she recalls a scripture. *"Now when they bring you to the synagogues and magistrates and authorities, do not worry about how or what you should answer, or what you should say. For the Holy Spirit will teach you in that very hour what you ought to say"* (Luke 12:11-12).

"Quiet, please!" a bailiff calls loudly. "Please be quiet. The court is now back in session."

The judge straightens his paperwork and places it neatly into one pile on the table in front of him.

"Is Rebekah Lynn Silver here?" The judge's eyes search the room.

Becky's body freezes at the sound of her name ringing throughout the courtroom. She wants to disappear and hide under the chair. . .anyplace where they won't find her. She feels nausea building up in the lining of her stomach. She squeezes her lips tight, fighting the urge to heave the Danish roll the guard gave her earlier that morning.

Before Becky can say a word the prosecutor speaks up. "Yes. The defendant Rebekah Lynn Silver is here."

"Thank you, counselor."

The prosecutor turns toward Becky. Earlier signs of victory have been erased from his face. "The World Union calls Rebekah Lynn Silver to the stand."

Lorraine reaches over and thoughtfully taps Becky on the leg. "God be with you, girl."

Becky feels everyone in the room staring at her. She can hear whispers and giggles around her. She wants the earth to open up and swallow her whole—she does not want to go before the judge or face that awful, loathsome attorney. She slowly stands to her feet. Her long white legs feel like jello. The shackles clang as she moves to the front of the room.

She stops in front of the very chair in which Brock denounced Jesus. The sight of it makes her skin turn cold.

"Please rise," the court clerk says loudly.

There is a clatter of chairs moving as everyone stands to their feet again.

"For the record," the clerk continues as the court reporter's fingers begin typing their quick motions on the keyboard, "the honorable Judge William Davis presides over case #RLS2450124, the World Union vs. Rebekah Lynn Silver. The defendant Rebekah Lynn Silver is on the stand. This court is now in session."

"You may sit down." The judge's hands are folded while his elbows rest on the table.

Becky slowly sits in the empty metal chair still warm from Brock's body. She tugs the hem of her shirt over her knees and folds her hands in her lap.

"For the record, please state your name," the prosecutor says in an informal tone as he approaches Becky.

"Re. . .Rebekah Silver." Her shoulders slouch forward.

"Rebekah, what do your friends call you, Rebekah or Becky?"

"Becky." She avoids his eyes.

"Okay, then, we shall call you Becky." He smiles warmly. "Becky, do you know why you are here?"

"I'm not sure," she says timidly.

The prosecutor walks over to the big oblong table and pulls a black book out of a black leather briefcase.

"Your Honor, please enter exhibit A." He briefly holds it up for the judge to see then walks back and hands it to Becky.

Becky accepts the book without looking up. She holds it gently in her lap and fondly traces the familiar gold letters with her finger, "Holy Bible."

"Becky, you are here today because you are accused of breaking one of our most important laws. Breaking this law is punishable by death."

He reaches out and gently places his forefinger under Becky's chin and lifts her face up toward his, forcing her to look into his eyes. "Do you understand what I'm saying, Becky?"

She nods.

"Counselor," the judge interrupts. "Do not touch the defendant!"

The attorney pulls his hand back. His face turns a shade of red. "I'm sorry, your honor. It won't happen again."

He stands tall, trying to compose himself. "Now where were we? Okay, for the record, please note that the defendant Rebekah Silver nodded her head yes."

The prosecutor turns toward the crowd then back to Becky. "Now, Becky, I want you to know we are not your enemies and we are here to help you. So please feel free to speak openly when you feel like speaking. You may ask me any question at any time if you like."

He reaches over and takes the Bible out of Becky's hands and places it on the table in front of the judge.

Clasping his fingers behind him he begins to stride back and forth. "Now isn't it true, Becky, that when you were living with your mother in Valencia you had secretly purchased the Bible on the internet and kept it hidden away?"

Becky keeps her eyes on the floor. "Yes, sir."

"Why then did you purchase a Bible on the internet if you knew owning a Bible was illegal and punishable by death?"

"I bought the Bible before Bibles were outlawed."

"So you bought the Bible before it was outlawed?"

"Yes, sir."

"So, Becky. . .after the Bibles were outlawed, did you turn your Bible in or get rid of it?"

"No."

"So you kept your Bible hidden away even after the World Union passed the law banning all Bibles?"

Becky doesn't answer. She keeps her eyes on the floor. Her mouth is dry, and her chapped lips are burning.

"Becky, do you know why the Bibles were outlawed?" He cocks his head to one side and regards Becky as a dim-witted child. "It is because man has distorted the truth of what God really meant to say. The Bible was never intended to be taken literally. The Bible is symbolic. This is why the World Union has replaced the old outdated Bible with 'The New Gospel.'"

He pauses for a moment then continues. "Becky, while you were in prison, were you given the book titled 'The New Gospel'?"

"Yes, sir."

"Well, good! If you read its precious teachings then you already know what a dramatic impact it can have on your life."

A wry smile creeps over her face as Becky recalls the pages of "The New Gospel" disappearing down the toilet in her cell.

"Do you have any questions about 'The New Gospel'?" She can feel his gaze boring into the side of her head.

"No, sir."

"Good! Now, Becky, we can be done with all this boring, legal stuff right now and you can go home to your mother if you will just acknowledge that Lord Maitreyas is the one and only Christ."

Becky swallows hard. "No, sir, I can't."

She hears gasps and loud whispers from the room.

The prosecutor stands and shoots a quick look of frustration to his assistant, who nods approvingly and continues writing feverishly on a long yellow notepad. He takes a breath and continues. "You're just a child, Becky.

How old are you, sixteen, seventeen?"

Becky has to think for a second. "Sixteen."

"So is all this just some kind of stupid teenage rebellious thing?" His words are harsh. "Are you trying to teach your mother some kind of a lesson? Because, really, no one can be this stupid!"

Snickers and laughs bounce off the walls.

"Order, please!" The judge looks disapprovingly as he hits the gavel on the table.

There is silence.

"Becky, all reasonable people can see that Lord Maitreyas is the true Christ. All of his predictions have come to pass; he has healed thousands of people and raised the dead, and even *he himself* has died and was resurrected." He kneels down and puts his face close to Becky's. "I know you aren't that stupid, Becky. Tell me, how can you look at all that Maitreyas has done and not believe in him?"

Becky speaks calmly. "Because Jesus said he is coming in the sky, 'as lightning flashes from the East to the West, so shall the coming of the Son of Man be.' He is coming in the clouds, and every eye will see him!"

"Yes, Becky, you are correct, but his coming in the sky is not literal but symbolic. Lord Maitreyas *has* fulfilled those prophecies. He *did* come back in the sky; he came unexpectedly 'like a thief in the night.' Don't you remember the great star that heralded Maitreyas's emergence? It was just like the star of Bethlehem that announced the birth of Jesus in his first initiation."

The people murmur in agreement. Becky's blood simmers as it rushes to her head. Her brows contract into a deep scowl, and she grits her teeth.

The prosecutor continues mechanically, as if reading from a script. "And on the Day of Pentecost, Maitreyas fulfilled the scriptures, 'every eye shall see him'! So you see, Becky, Lord Maitreyas has passed every test you can think of. He has proven beyond any doubt that he is the

Christ."

Becky suddenly lurches forward, fire in her eyes. "MAITREYAS IS NOT THE CHRIST!" Her voice cracks as she shrieks at the top of her lungs. The judge jumps back in his chair, startled by her sudden outburst. "He is the Antichrist. He's tricked you. He has tricked all of you." She stares out at the faces in the room who stare back in disbelief. "His name equals six-six-six. The Bible warned us he would come. It warned us that his name would equal six-six-six. He is not our savior. He is the beast of Revelation!"

Offended gasps ripple in the air. Several people stand and gesture violently at Becky.

"Death to the resister!" someone shouts.

"Execute the traitor!" says another.

Tap, tap, tap, tap, tap. The court reporter beats at the electronic keyboard.

"Order! Order now!" The judge bangs his hammer on the table. "I will clear this courtroom if I don't have order now." The judge shoots a disdainful look at Becky, this insolent little girl who dares to try to turn his courtroom into a circus. The room suddenly falls silent. He nods at the prosecutor to continue.

"Becky," the prosecutor says in a calm voice, appearing not to be bothered by the earlier outburst. "The beast John was referring to in Revelation was the emperor Nero. He was the one persecuting Christians at the time John wrote those letters. And when you translate 'Nero Caesar' into Hebrew letters, his name equals six-six-six. So you see, Becky, Nero was the beast John was writing about. And besides lots of people have names that equal six-six-six. Are all of them the so-called Antichrist too?" Soft laughter comes from behind him. "But"—he maintains a dead-pan expression and continues—"I mean, I'm sure there is some wild, superstitious calculation that can be applied to your own name that would render the dreaded number six-six-six. That doesn't make you the Antichrist, does it?"

He carefully adjusts a dark strand of hair that dangles near his left eye. "The scriptures said there were many antichrists in the world. The truth, Becky—the truth you must accept—is that the Antichrist is not a person at all. It is a force, a destructive energy that has worked its evil through the disasters that have plagued our world since the beginning of time. Earthquakes, tornados, hurricanes, tsunamis, drought and the starvation of millions of people are all the works of the antichrist energy.

"Again, reasonable people can see this as proof that Maitreyas is in fact the true Christ, because, as we have all seen, only *he* can overpower this energy."

A sullen look covers Becky's face. Her lips tighten, and her forehead frowns. *Help me, Lord,* she prays silently. *I need you, and I need you now. . . .*

"Becky!"

"Huh? Would you please repeat the question?"

"I *said* even the ascended master Peter Roma has said that Lord Maitreyas is the Christ! How can you deny that?"

Becky shifts her shoulders back and sits up straight. Her eyes focus directly up at the intimidating man standing in front of her. "Because Peter Roma is *not* the same Jesus of Nazareth." She speaks slowly and confidently. "He is an imposter and a liar! Peter Roma is one of the fallen rebellious angels who were cast out of heaven with Satan. He is the false prophet of Revelation!

"And Peter Roma claims that as Jesus he was crucified and resurrected. Then I ask, where are his scars? He has no scars because he is *not* Jesus. He is a *fake* and a *liar!* The *real* Jesus of Nazareth has scars because he was *nailed* to the cross on Calvary! The *real* Jesus of Nazareth, who died more than two thousand years ago, is the one and only Christ, not Maitreyas!

"The Bible says, 'Jesus is the Christ, the Son of the living God,' and there are 333 fulfilled Bible prophecies that *prove* that Jesus of Nazareth is the Christ!"

She stops for a moment to catch her breath and deeply inhales the stale air. She struggles to organize the thoughts and scriptures flooding her mind. The prosecutor parts his tight lips, but before he can utter a syllable Becky continues.

"'In the beginning was the Word, and the Word was with God, and the Word was God. . .and the Word became flesh. . .and dwelt among us.'

"'Jesus Christ is the same yesterday and today and forever.'

"'Therefore also God highly exalted him and bestowed on him the name which is above every name, that at the name of *Jesus* every knee should bow, of those who are in heaven and on earth and under the earth and that every tongue should confess that 'Jesus Christ is Lord' to the glory of God the Father!'"

She stops. Her breath is fast and shallow, as if she has just finished a hundred-yard sprint. She stares at the prosecutor, ready to deflect any salvo he fires back at her.

"Oh, brother," murmurs a black-haired young man in the front row, his words cut short by a dirty look from the judge.

Frustrated, the prosecutor's eyes look up and to the left as he pauses like a laptop computer downloading a large file.

"Becky, didn't you read 'The New Gospel'?"

"Uh. . .yeah. . .a little bit."

"Well, if you *did* read it, then you would know why Peter Roma has no scars. It is because he has ascended with a new body."

Becky sighs. *Now he's starting to sound like Momma.*

"You see, Becky, Peter Roma is an enlightened master. Let me explain: There are five expansions of consciousness, which makes a man an enlightened master

163

by symbolically going through each of them. Jesus' birth in Bethlehem symbolized the first initiation. I won't explain all of them, but when Jesus was crucified this symbolized the fourth initiation. Three days after Jesus died it was the Christ Maitreyas who entered his body, and it was the Christ Maitreyas who resurrected his body. This symbolized the fifth initiation."

The prosecutor smiles to himself when he realizes he has everyone's utmost attention. He continues. "Jesus became a master of wisdom when he achieved the fifth initiation. In his next incarnation he was born as Apollonius of Tyana. As Apollonius he ascended with a new body therefore erasing his scars. History tells us he traveled to India where he died and was buried there. This is where the confusion comes in about Jesus not dying on the cross."

Becky feels her energy draining as the prosecutor rambles on.

"So in his last and final incarnation Peter Roma has ascended with yet another new body. So you see, Becky, that is why he has no scars."

The prosecutor's hands rest on his hips. "Becky, it is Lord Maitreyas's will that you choose him and choose life. If you deny him, Lord Maitreyas will deny you.

"And remember, Becky, if you deny Lord Maitreyas, it is *not* Lord Maitreyas who condemns you to death. It is your own doing."

He bends his knees and squats down beside Becky's chair, careful not to touch her, and looks directly into her eyes. In a kind and soft tone he says, "I plead with you, Becky. Do the smart and sensible thing. *Live* and choose Christ Lord Maitreyas."

He stands back to his feet. Becky recognizes the same posture he had taken when he called on Brock to make his decision.

"For the record, Becky"—he pronounces each word loudly—"what is your decision?"

The very air in the courtroom seems to wait for her to speak. Everyone's eyes stare at her in a quizzical manner. Their shoulders are hunched, leaning forward, waiting for her answer.

She glances at the red-headed newspaper reporter, who called himself Bob Brown, seated in the front row. His eyes prod her, and he mouths the words "Choose Maitreyas."

She looks toward the back row and sees Lorraine, her eyes closed and her hands folded tightly together. She realizes Lorraine is praying for her. All the prisoners are praying, their hands knit together. A loud clang breaks the tense silence as one prisoner's shackles rub against the metal folding chair as he raises his hands up toward heaven.

She suddenly feels a strong supernatural power. Her skin begins to feel cool, and goose bumps blanket her arms. She swallows as she chokes back tears. She feels the overwhelming presence of God and his holy angels near her. She can almost see them, surrounding her, protecting her and whispering words of comfort in her ears. A sense of peace fills her innermost being. She sits up straight and lifts her chin, proudly.

"I choose Jesus Christ of Nazareth, King of kings and Lord of lords, whom God sent down to earth to die for our sins, who has scars from when he was nailed to the cross and who was resurrected three days later and who now sits at the right hand of God. For if I die with him, I shall also live with him. If I endure, I shall also reign with him. If I deny him, he also will deny me. If I am faithless, he remains faithful; for he cannot deny himself. I choose Jesus Christ, the Son of the living God!"

"Praise Jesus!" a prisoner yells from the back row.

The prosecutor huffs in disgust. "Well, Becky." His voice is cold and harsh. "I can see that you have been brainwashed. I cannot do any more for you."

He steps up to the table and speaks impatiently to the judge. "Your honor, the World Union requests permission to strike that last paragraph."

Surprised, the judge turns to the court reporter. "Renee, please read back to me the last paragraph."

Renee tugs at the roll of tape in the stenotype machine. She twists strands of hair with her fingers as she reads aloud the transcript. "I choose Jesus Christ of Nazareth, King of kings, Lord—"

"Stop there!" the judge interrupts. "Strike the paragraph after the sentence, 'I choose Jesus Christ of Nazareth." The judge frowns. "Is that all, counselor?"

"Yes, sir. Thank you, sir." He walks to the table where his assistant has already begun assembling the files for the next case. "The World Union rests, your honor."

The judge picks up an ink pen and scribbles on a sheet of paper. He makes a fist with his right hand and covers his mouth to clear his throat.

"Will the defendant Rebekah Lynn Silver please stand."

Becky takes a deep breath and slowly pulls herself out of the hard, metal chair. She stands to a full five-foot seven inches; her tattered orange shirt rests slightly below her knees. With her hands bound together she holds her head high, her ponytail dangling in the middle of her back.

"The court finds the defendant Rebekah Lynn Silver"—the judge's voice is gruff—"guilty beyond a reasonable doubt on all three counts under article 130 of the World Union Constitution.

"Count one: W.U. 130.28. 'Any person or persons having in their possession, and or on the premises of their home, any translation of the Christian Bible part or in full; printed, electronic, or audio, shall be put to death.'

"Count two: W.U. 130 (a). 'The following shall include all person or persons over the age of one year, section (43), any person or persons refusing a World Union approved microchip implant with Christ Maitreyas's name, his number or his mark[28] inserted on his or her right hand or forehead shall be put to death.

"Count three: W.U. 130.42. 'Any person or persons refusing to bow down to Christ Maitreyas or any graven image of Christ Maitreyas shall be put to death.'

"The court hereby sentences Rebekah Lynn Silver to death by beheading with the guillotine today at 6:00 P.M., on the lawn behind this World Union courthouse."

The judge places the papers into a manila file and hands the file to the clerk. He slams his gavel on the table and stands. "The court will now adjourn for lunch until 1:00 P.M. I'm famished!"

Then they will deliver you up to tribulation and kill you, and you will be hated by all nations for my name's sake.
Matthew 24:9

Blessed are those who are persecuted for righteousness' sake, for theirs is the kingdom of heaven. Blessed are you when they revile and persecute you, and say all kinds of evil against you falsely for my sake. Rejoice and be exceedingly glad, for great is your reward in heaven, for so they persecuted the prophets who were before you.
Matthew 5:10-12

---

[28] "He causes all, both small and great, rich and poor, free and slave, to receive a mark on their right hand or on their foreheads, and that no one may buy or sell except one who has the mark or the name of the beast, or the number of his name" (Revelation 13:16-17).

8

THE EXECUTION

With her wrists and ankles shackled, Becky takes tiny steps as two black-hooded executioners, one on each side, grip her elbows firmly and escort her down the long narrow hallway. Their boots fall heavily on the floor alongside Becky's bare feet.

They stop before the glass exit doors and wait as the W.U. guard on the other side pulls the aluminum handle and holds the door open. They pass through to the outside and slowly descend concrete steps and into the courtyard.

Tall steel-and-glass buildings pierce the gloomy grey-and-red skyline, while a giant World Union flag snaps and flutters lazily in a warm evening breeze.

"'Yea, though I walk through the valley of the shadow of death, I will fear no evil, for thou art with me,'" Becky whispers under her breath as they move forward. Water pools in the corners of her eyes.

Several people huddle together holding signs and waving small World Union flags. Large, garish silver jewelry jiggles from their pierced ears, lips and noses. A rowdy group of young men whose heads are shaved descend the steps and immediately begin chanting, "Death to the resister! Long live Christ Maitreyas!"

A large, black-haired lady smiles while waving a red flag bearing a black silhouette of Maitreyas high over her head. Her face is painted blue and white, the colors of the World Union. Next to her, a boy no older than six holds a poster board over his head that reads, "Resisters are the cancer. Maitreyas is the answer."

A hand-scrawled sign catches Becky's eyes. She reads, "Behead all who insult Christ Maitreyas."

"Ugh!" It feels like someone has just socked her in the stomach. "I can't believe this is happening. Lord Jesus. . .come quickly!" she mumbles.

On a rough-hewn wood platform erected in the middle of the courtyard, beckoning its next victim, sits the "death machine," its broad razor-sharp blade mocking those, reminding them of their doom if they refuse to worship Maitreyas.

Adjacent to the guillotine sits a statue[29], a smaller version of the five-hundred-foot bronze Maitreyas statue in India. It is an image of Maitreyas sitting on his throne, his left hand resting on his leg while his right hand is held up in the air, his third and fourth fingers slightly forward. "Maitreyas the Christ, Lord of Love" is engraved in marble at the base of the throne, and below that, "Maitreyas, Messiah, Krishna, Imam Mahdi and World Teacher."

Flowers and candles litter the base of the giant statue. Small scraps of paper, held down by stones and pebbles, bear the hopeful prayers of worshippers who visit the statue regularly.

Becky shakes her head sadly as she pictures Brock kneeling before the bronze beast, sealing his fate for

---

[29] "That they should make an image to the beast, which had the wound by a sword, and did live" (Revelation 13:14).

eternity.

"It's not too late," the hooded man to Becky's left whispers in a gritty, low voice. "Peter Roma has ordered statues in front of every guillotine, because it's never too late. You can always repent and worship Lord Maitreyas."

"Corporal, remain silent!" Becky feels the glove on her right arm tighten as the second executioner reprimands the one on her left.

"Yes, sir." She hears the man to her left take a deep breath beneath his hood. "I just thought. . . ."

"Save yourself!" shouts a teenage girl dressed in black, gothic-style clothes. A black X[30] is boldly tattooed on her forehead. "Worship Lord Maitreyas the Christ!"

Terror rips through Becky's soul as the men stop in front of the steps of the guillotine. With an anguished groan she looks toward the orange and purple sky one last time. Salty tears gently course down her innocent cheeks. She tries to ignore the crushing weight that has leeched itself upon her chest.

One of the executioners stops and releases her elbow as the other turns her body toward the sturdy stairs that lead up to her demise.

Becky and the hooded man slowly ascend the steps. Her throat is dry, and it feels like someone is strangling her. Her ankle shackles clang as they step onto the platform. She looks down at her feet; the wood is stained brownish-red.

Her eyes dart back and forth from the executioner to the crowd to the silver blade hanging high above. The smell of stale blood lingers like perfume in the dry air. She shudders as she wonders how many people have died here before her.

Wood splinters dig into her skin as the executioner pushes her down to her knees. His black leather glove grasps her ponytail and guides her head through the notch

---

[30]   Chi (X) Xi Stigma is 666 in Greek. "X" also means Christ.

of the guillotine and rests her neck on the wooden slot. He secures the brace.

She leans her shoulders forward against the wood to release the pressure that is pinching her back.

She squeezes her eyes shut, blocking out the statue of Maitreyas and the jeering crowd gathered to watch her die.

She silently mouths the words, *For if I die with him, I shall also live with him. If I endure, I shall also reign with him. If I deny him, he also will deny me.*

Her head spins, like a Ferris wheel spiraling out of control. She whimpers an urgent prayer. "Lord Jesus. . .please help me! Please help me to be strong. . . .

Focus, focus on Jesus, she tells herself repeatedly.

In her mind she pictures Jesus, his half-naked limp body mangled from the countless hours of whipping and beating. He dangles high from long rusty nails hammered into a hefty splintered stake. Flies collect on the crossbeam where red ooze trickles down from his pierced hands. They buzz around the droplets of bloody sweat from his forehead as it streams down his puffy black-and-blue face and pools in his matted beard.

She imagines herself looking up into his sorrowful bloodshot eyes. She hears him groan in sheer agony as he turns away and lifts his weary head up to heaven and says, "Father, if it is your will, take this cup away from me; nevertheless not my will, but yours, be done."

Her chest aches as she feels his pain.

She writhes in discomfort as the wood brace pinches down hard on her neck. She tries to twist her head but is only welcomed by a nagging, gnawing pain.

"I can do all things through Christ who strengthens me," she says as she forces her tormented mind away from that atrocious metal blade that will come crashing down on her neck separating her head from her body at any moment.

"Lord Jesus," she whispers, "please let it be quick, and please, don't let it hurt. . . ."

There is silence.

She feels a light tap on her shoulder.

She ignores it.

Focus on Jesus. . .focus. . . .

There it is again.

Have they changed their minds? she wonders.

The tapping turns into a tug. Someone has grabbed her elbow and is pulling her up to her feet.

Her eyelids flutter open.

Her gaze is met by a tall incredibly beautiful angelic being. His clear blue eyes twinkle as he smiles warmly down upon her.

Puzzled, her eyes cast down to see her crumpled beheaded body lying lifeless on the wood platform, crimson blood oozing from the neck.

Am I dead? But. . .but I never felt the deadly blade. If my body is dead. . .then my spirit[31] must still be alive!

"Becky," says the angel, a luminous aura surrounding his blond curly hair. "Come with me."

In a transport of delight she follows the angel down the steps onto the sunburned grass, his long white robe flowing gracefully behind him.

The crowd of people gathered to watch the execution is now dispersing and scattering throughout the courtyard.

Tears stream down the face of a hunched-over, grey-haired woman clutching a cane as she shakes her head in grief. "Poor, poor child. May God rest her soul."

Skateboards tucked under their arms and their baseball caps turned backward, two smiling boys strain

---

[31] "It is sown a natural body; it is raised a spiritual body. There is a natural body, and there is a spiritual body" (1 Corinthians 15:44).

their necks to get a look at the motionless body.[32] "Oh, man, cool." They cackle, emitting loud inarticulate noises. "Look at all that blood!"

People chant, "Long live Lord Maitreyas! Long live the Christ!" as they wave their World Union flags in approval of what they have just witnessed.

The crowds pass within inches of Becky as she stands on the courtyard lawn. She realizes that although she can see them they do not see her.

The angel stops. He reaches for her hand and gently tucks it under his left arm. She smiles as she feels the silky robes wrap around her arm.

The angel lifts his chin up toward heaven and extends his right hand in the air. Suddenly a massive beam of light parts the sky, like a zipper, to show darkness, and then out of the darkness thousands of equidistant bursts of meteoric explosions of light appear. It is like a flashlight shining across a room on high beam.

Their feet slowly lift off the ground as they are drawn into the tunnel of light. Becky is astounded as she tries to absorb everything that is happening to her. She cannot stop herself from smiling.

Together they traverse through the shimmering white tunnel at speeds Becky cannot comprehend, cutting through the dark space that surrounds the earth toward the third heaven.

Becky gasps as a brilliant halo of clouds emerges,

---

[32] "And they overcame him by the blood of the Lamb, and by the word of their testimony; and they loved not their lives unto the death" (Revelation 12:11).

displaying a magnificent spectrum of violet, blue, orange and red ice crystals.

"We are almost there," the angel says reassuringly.

The colorful clouds part to expose a bright yellow metallic stairwell that extends upward.

They slowly descend to the base of the stairwell. *Is this heaven?* Becky wonders as her feet touch a hard transparent floor.

The angel gently squeezes Becky's hand as he takes it off his arm. "Follow the steps." His finger points up the stairs.

Her eyes look up at the giant stairwell of lovely golden steps, white clouds hovering about.

She lifts her leg to take a step. She takes another step and another. Step after step she climbs the stairs through the clouds. As she takes each step, she notices the golden steps seem to grow bigger and she grows smaller, like a child.

She climbs and climbs. Her skin feels warm as though the sun is shining on it. She inhales deeply and smiles at the scent of lilacs and roses, jasmine and honeysuckle.

She continues climbing and climbing. Step after step.

The clouds begin radiating more and more brilliant rays of light.

Her eyes are wild with exaltation as she comes to the end of the stairwell. She gazes down to see her reflection on a sea of transparent glass, like flawless diamonds mixed with orange and yellow flames. "Wow!" She beams excitedly.

Her eyes look up and focus on a beautiful bow of red, orange, yellow, green, blue, indigo and violet, illuminating over a large emerald throne that is grander than anything she has ever seen before. She is amazed at the beautiful colors waltzing through the air.

Waves of orange and yellow ripple below her feet

like waves of fire as she sets her foot on the transparent glass.

Her small frame slowly moves toward the giant throne. Her heart speeds, and she catches her breath. She sees that a Man of great stature is sitting on the throne, great beams of light emanating from his body like the sun.

She pushes herself closer. Exultant happiness fills the depths of her soul as she recognizes the Man wearing the bright, lamb-white robe, a golden sash draped across his broad chest, so glorious and magnificent!

She suddenly realizes this is the moment—the most important moment in her whole tiny existence—she is standing face-to-face with the Creator of the universe.

She is overwhelmed by his intense beauty and the splendor of his presence; goose bumps swallow her, and her body becomes weak. Her legs buckle beneath her, and she tumbles to the floor shielding her face with her arm.

"Do not be afraid, My child." His strong voice echoes through the jewel-studded air.

Becky's hand slips away from her face.

He is leaning forward, his snow-white hair reflecting red, yellow and blue. He stretches his right hand toward her, beckoning her to come forward.

Slowly she stands and moves toward him. She reaches up and places her tiny hand inside his large outstretched hand.

His hand is so soft and warm. Becky's body trembles in awe, and yet she sighs as she relaxes in his strong grasp. A puzzled look crosses her face as she feels something rough in the smooth cup of his hand.

She peers closer to get a better look.

Suddenly her eyes sparkle, and her smile stretches from ear to ear. She places her thin, delicate fingers inside his hand and strokes his beautiful, jagged scar, formed more than two thousand years ago when he was nailed to the cross.

She looks up into his gentle fiery eyes. He smiles lovingly down at her and says, "I am the living one." Diamonds, rubies and sapphires encrust the wide band that forms the base of his gold crown. "I was dead, and, behold, I am alive, forever and ever!"

He carefully lifts her up onto his lap and wraps both of his arms around her small shoulders. She feels his breath against her cheek. He squeezes her tight as a father squeezes his child after being away for a long while. He strokes her golden-blond locks and whispers softly in her ear, "Well done, Rebekah, My child, well done!"

Then I saw the souls of those who had been beheaded for their witness to Jesus and for the word of God, who had not worshiped the beast or his image and had not received his mark on their foreheads or on their hands. And they lived and reigned with Christ for a thousand years.
Revelation 20:4

These are the ones who come out of the great tribulation, washed their robes and made them white in the blood of the Lamb. Therefore they are before the throne of God and serve him day and night in his temple. And he who sits on the throne will dwell among them. They shall neither hunger anymore nor thirst anymore; the sun shall not strike them, nor any heat; for the Lamb who is in the midst of the throne will shepherd them and lead them to living fountains of waters. And God will wipe away every tear from their eyes.
Revelation 7:14-17

Dear Friend,

Many of you are aware of the coming antichrist and say that you will **not** worship him or take his mark. The Bible says **you will** if your name is not written in the Book of Life.

"And all that dwell upon the earth shall worship him, whose names are not written in the book of life of the Lamb slain from the foundation of the world"
(Revelation 13:8).

Some of you may ask, "So how do I get my name in the Lamb's book of life?"

The Bible says, "That if thou shalt confess with thy mouth the Lord Jesus, and shalt believe in thine heart that God hath raised him from the dead, thou shalt be saved. For with the heart man believeth unto righteousness; and with the mouth confession is made unto salvation"
(Romans 10:9-10).

Don't wait another second; accept Jesus as your Lord and Savior before it's too late. . . .

Blessings,

Patience Prence

Dear Reader,

If you have been touched by *SCARS,* please refer this book to your pastor, church, family and friends. You may also log on to www.amazon.com and give your review. This will help Amazon recommend *SCARS* to other readers in the Amazon community. A five-star review would be greatly appreciated!

You can also give *SCARS* as a gift, or please consider sharing your thoughts about this book on a website or blog—but please don't give away the plot!

Please visit our website at www.thespringharvest.com for *SCARS* WORD SEARCH puzzle and *SCARS* quiz and current news.

Thank you and God bless you!

ACKNOWLEDGMENTS

First I would like to acknowledge and thank my mother Judith—without her help this book would not be the exciting dramatized novel it is. She believed in the book and inspired me to keep pressing forward.

Jessica, whose enthusiasm encouraged me after she read the very first draft and said it was the best, most exciting book she'd ever read.

I would like to thank Cousin Ray for his time and expert advice. His writing professionalism quite surpassed all expectations.

Debbie, who did a superb job in editing and for all of her many ideas and suggestions.

Edward, my artist friend who helped me with the cover design. If anyone needs great artwork, please contact Spring Harvest for Ed's email.

LambCreek for the beautiful layout.

I would also like to thank all of my family and friends for reading my many drafts and for their support—James, Dad, Imelda, Nancy, Susan, Tamara and Rebekah.

And last but not least I want to thank my loving husband Dennis for his patience and help throughout this journey.

I thank you and love you all!

Patience Prence

HOW TO ORDER ONLINE

To order this book online, go to www.amazon.com or www.amazon.co.uk and select "Books" from the Amazon category menu, and then enter Patience Prence in the search box. On the page that comes up, click on the books title "SCARS" to access details and ordering information.

You may also follow the link at www.thespringharvest.com

Thank you!

AUTHOR

Patience Prence is a gifted writer who was fascinated by the book of Revelation as a young child. She has studied Revelation and end-time prophecies for many years. A lifelong Christian and businesswoman, she orients her research and knowledge toward helping others understand God's Word.

Patience suffers from Usher Syndrome, a disease that causes blindness (Retinitis Pigmentosa) and hearing loss.

You may visit Patience's website at:

www.thespringharvest.com/patienceprence/

CPSIA information can be obtained at www.ICGtesting.com
Printed in the USA
LVOW11s0852170416

484012LV00001B/320/P